all the things you are

Also by Courtney Sheinmel

Sincerely

Positively

My So-Called Family

all the things you are

Courtney Sheinmel

Simon & Schuster Books for Young Readers
New York London Toronto Sydney

SIMON & SCHUSTER BOOKS FOR YOUNG READERS
An imprint of Simon & Schuster Children's Publishing Division
1230 Avenue of the Americas, New York, New York 10020
This book is a work of fiction. Any references to historical events, real people, or real locales are used fictitiously. Other names, characters, places, and incidents are products of the author's imagination, and any resemblance to actual events or locales or persons, living or dead, is entirely coincidental.

Book design by Krista Vossen
The text for this book is set in Baskerville.
Manufactured in the United States of America • 0511 FFG
2 4 6 8 10 9 7 5 3 1
Library of Congress Cataloging-in-Publication Data
Sheinmel, Courtney.
All the things you are / Courtney Sheinmel. —1st ed.
p. cm.
Summary: When Carly Wheeler's mother is arrested for embezzling from the soap opera where she works, Carly's perfect life begins to fall apart as her friends at her prestigious private school stop talking to her, her beloved stepfather starts worrying about finances, and her image of herself and her family changes.
ISBN 978-1-4169-9717-7 (hardcover)
ISBN 978-1-4169-9719-1 (eBook)
[1. Embezzlement—Fiction. 2. Family problems—Fiction. 3. Friendship—Fiction. 4. Stepfamilies—Fiction. 5. Conduct of life—Fiction. 6. Westchester County (N.Y.)—Fiction.] I. Title.
PZ7.S54124Al 2011
[Fic]—dc22
2010010090

For Phil Getter, a.k.a. Faux Pa

And for IanMichael, Laura & Doug

xoxox

acknowledgments

Thank you:

To my agent, Alex Glass, for saying "You have to write that!" as soon as I told him the idea, and for his encouragement and friendship at every step along the way; and to my editor, David Gale, for giving this book a home and for taking such good care of the things I write.

To Lara Allen, Kate Crockett, and Adam Friedstein at Trident Media Group; and to Justin Chanda, Paul Crichton, Bernadette Cruz, Katrina Groover, Michelle Kratz, Chrissy Noh, Nicole Russo, Karen Sherman, Krista Vossen, and Navah Wolfe—my heroes at Simon & Schuster.

To my friends, the most extraordinary group of people I've ever known: Amy Bressler and Arielle Warshall Katz, who oftentimes seem to understand the things in my head even better than I do, and who know exactly when I need reassurance and when I need to be pushed forward; to Lindsay Aaronson, Samantha Anobile, Amanda Berlin, Maria Crocitto, Jenn Daly, Denise, Alan, Courtney & Morgan Fleischman, Gayle Forman, Jackie Friedland, Jake Glaser, Mary Gordon, Daphne Grab, Regan Hofmann, Allyson Jaron Haas, Lisa, Peter, Marachel & Lily Leib, Logan Levkoff, Melissa Losquadro, Wendy Mass, Christine Moyers, Llen Pomeroy, Stacia, Luc, Jessarae Robitaille & Steven R. McQueen, Jennie Rosenberg, Rebecca & Jeremy Wallace-Segall, Eric, Madden & Brody Shuffler and Katie Stein, whose collective continued support makes me weep with gratitude; and to Steven Sparling, who gave me a refresher course on legal concepts and the criminal justice system (and who helped name *Lovelock Falls*).

acknowledgments

To Carly Simon, whose music I've listened to and loved for as long as I can remember, and whose voice is the most perfect and comforting thing to have in the background as I'm writing.

And, as always, to my wonderful family—Mom, Dad, Grandma Doris, Lyss & JP; and to my own fabulous "faux" family—Phil Getter, IanMichael Getter, Suncica, Doug, Sara & Tesa Getter and Laura, Rob, Nicki, Andrew & Zach Liss. Thank you for always being there—your belief in me makes me believe in myself.

My love to you all,
Courtney

all the things you are

chapter one

For the past three years my best friend, Annie, and I have had the coolest tradition on Teacher Organization Day.

I guess I should explain what Teacher Organization Day even is: It's this random day at the end of September when classes are canceled and the teachers have a day to catch up on their work. I really don't get the reason for it; honestly, I think it's just an excuse for the school administration to have a three-day weekend. We go to a private school called Preston Day School. Tuition is pretty steep, which goes along with my stepfather's theory that the more you pay for a school, the more vacation days you get. He may be right about that—my stepsister and stepbrother go to public school, and they never have days off for things like Teacher Organization Day. Also, their winter and spring breaks are shorter, and their school gets out two weeks after ours does in June. But whatever the reason, I'm not going to complain about it. All that matters to me is that we have that Monday off.

So this is our tradition: My mom takes Annie and me to work with her. We've been doing it ever since the fourth grade.

I know it doesn't sound like much of a tradition. Actually, it probably sounds lame to hang out at the place where your mother works, and maybe that's how it would be if you were going to *your* mother's office. But my mom has a job where it's cool to go for the day—in fact she has the coolest job of all the parents I know. She works on the set of the soap opera *Lovelock Falls*.

In case you haven't heard of it, Lovelock Falls is a made-up town, and the show is about all the people who live there. It's filmed in Manhattan, which is about an hour away from where we live. When we go, the crew totally treats us like we're celebrities ourselves. We get to go to the hair and makeup room and get made up just like the actors do, and then we watch the filming and the set changes. In between scenes the real actors come up and talk to us, and we get our pictures taken with everyone. They also have this area called Craft Services, where there's so much food you can't even believe it. Basically, any kind of dish you can imagine is there—including tons of desserts. I sort of wonder how all the actresses on the show stay so super thin, since they can eat at Craft Services all day long. But I think they have personal trainers.

Mom is a stylist on *Lovelock Falls*, and she handles the wardrobe for six of the women on the show, including the star, Ally Jaron. Ally plays Violet van Ryan. So far she's been almost murdered twice, been in a coma, and had four different weddings—two of them to the same guy. His character, Kyle Shepherd, has amnesia right now, so he doesn't even remember that she left him for the second time, right after she found out that he was a compulsive gambler and had gambled away most of her fortune. Violet also has ten-year-old twins, and one of them just came back from the dead. And she has a twin sister herself, but Violet's twin sister, Ivy, is evil, and Ivy got shipped off to an insane asylum last year.

Of course, Ally isn't anything like that in real life. Mom says the cast and crew of *Lovelock Falls* are like family, and she knows them all really well. I know Ally too, because Mom has worked with her for so long. Her house isn't too far from where my family lives, and I've visited her with Mom. When I had appendicitis last year, Ally sent me a care package filled with DVDs and magazines. It's not really intimidating to be around her, because she's so completely down-to-earth. She has two daughters, Madison and Nicole, who are super cute. They look so much like Ally that it's crazy—blondish hair and really wide blue-green eyes. They remind me of dolls. I've babysat for them a couple of times, and even though I don't think of Ally as a star, I have to admit that it was cool to see the inside of her house—maybe not as cool as getting to see where a movie star like Brody Hudson lives, but still. The table next to the couch in the living room has a bunch of framed pictures on it—pictures of Ally and her friends, who just happen to be famous themselves. And she has a huge walk-in closet right off her bedroom. There are all these photos on the walls of her dressed up in spectacular designer gowns.

Mom says Ally is a really easy person to dress because she has a great sense of style and everything looks good on her. In the scene she was filming that day, she was wearing a flowing dress that stopped just below her knees. It had a halter top—the halter part was crocheted, and then the bottom of the dress was sort of silky. It was a bunch of different colors that you wouldn't necessarily think would go well together, but somehow they just did. I think the truth is that my mom is really good at her job—she's just so stylish herself. She's personable, and she knows how to make people feel really good about themselves so they always like what they're wearing. Mom has even been nominated for a bunch of different awards for dressing the actresses so well. We have the nomination certificates framed in our den.

The funniest thing about the wardrobe on *Lovelock Falls* is that all the actors are always dressed up in really fancy clothes, no matter where the scene takes place, as if at any moment they might need to dash off to a black-tie event. That day Violet van Ryan was at the hospital to visit her ex-husband—the one with amnesia. But she looked like she was ready to be a guest at a wedding. Annie and I were in directors' chairs just to the side of the set, so we had a good view. One of the crew gave us headsets so we could listen to the dialogue.

"Well, Dr. Sparling, that is just unacceptable," Ally-as-Violet said. "I expect you to have a different answer when I come back tomorrow, or else I am pulling the foundation's funding of the new wing, and in case you don't know what that will mean, I will tell you: It will be a disaster of epic proportions. It will change all—all the things you are." She turned around quickly and stormed off. Her dress swayed back and forth, the colors blending together just right. She looked glamorous and intense all at once.

"Cut!" the director said.

The scene was over, so Ally came over to us. "Hey, Carly," she said, hugging me hello.

"Hi," I said. "Do you remember Annie? She comes with me every year."

"Sure," she said. "Hi, Annie."

Ally extended her hand for Annie to shake. I happen to know that Ally doesn't like her hands. She thinks the veins in them make her look old. She taught me this trick that if you hold your hands so your fingers are pointed upward, you can't see the veins as well, and it makes your hands look younger. Annie shook Ally's hand. I could tell she was jealous that Ally had hugged me and not her. I know it's mean, but it made me sort of glad. At school Annie is definitely more popular than I am. She has this personality that just makes her stand out and sparkle. I'm lucky to be her best friend, but all the same it's nice to feel like the important one sometimes.

"How do you think the scene went?" Ally asked.

"It was great," I said.

"Are you sure?" Ally asked. "I screwed up a couple of the lines and I had to improvise." She seemed genuinely worried, even though she's been playing Violet van Ryan for years and years. She's really good at it, too. I think she's probably the best actress on *Lovelock Falls*.

"It sounded completely natural," Annie said. "It was just how I would have done the scene." Annie is actually in drama club at school, and every time we visit the set, she hopes she'll be discovered—like the director will decide that he really needs a twelve-year-old in a certain scene, and that Annie has the perfect look. She says a lot of really famous people got their start on the soaps. Whenever we talk about what we want to be when we grow up, Annie says she should be an actress and I should be a writer. Her plan is that I will be a writer on a soap opera, since I'm good at making up stories and I know a lot about the soaps, and I'll write her a really great part.

"Seriously," I told Ally, "you totally nailed it."

Ally ruffled my hair. "Thanks, girls," she said. "I've got to run—I have to make an appearance at a benefit downtown. I can't even remember if it's for the museum or the library. It's the third night in a row I've had one of these things. I promised the girls I'd be home in time to put them to bed, but I don't know if I'll really make it. You know, it's really hard to be a good mother. I look at how Leigh is with you, Carly. I just hope in the end I'm the same kind of mother she is."

I love when Ally talks to me like I'm her friend. "You're a good mother too," I said.

"My guru says I need to work on simplifying my life," Ally said.

Here's something else about Ally: You can't really know her without hearing what her guru says. It's the one sort of weird thing about her. Her guru is this guy from India who teaches her yoga and meditation. He says all sorts of things, like life is full of signs—you just need to watch for them—and there's no such thing as a mistake. I'm not sure I believe that last one; just last week I messed up on my math quiz even when I really knew the answer, and I certainly didn't do it on purpose.

"Madison and Nicole are worried that if I simplify too

much, they'll end up with fewer toys," she continued.

I smiled, because the girls have so many toys. It's practically a toy store at Ally's house. "Tell them I say hi," I said.

"I will," Ally said. "Come visit us soon—actually, maybe the weekend after next your mom can bring you by. I have a lunch thing, and I know the girls would rather play with you than tag along with their old mom."

"That sounds good," I said.

After Ally left, Annie and I headed back to my mom's office. Mom calls it her office, but really it's just a cluttered room that she shares with a few of the other stylists. There are racks of clothing everywhere, and labels taped to the hangers so they know who is supposed to wear which outfit in what scene. A couple of times I've seen actresses walking around Mom's office without clothes on. They don't seem to care who sees them, but I would definitely be more self-conscious. I'm kind of a late bloomer. I guess it's obvious even when I have clothes on that I'm totally flat-chested, but it's not like I ever want anyone to see it up close.

I pushed open the door to Mom's office. There was a rack of dresses right in front of the door—I couldn't see Mom through them, but I could hear her talking to Vivette. Vivette is the head stylist, so she's sort of Mom's boss, but she doesn't act like a boss at all. She and Mom are really good friends. Vivette and her husband, Ed, always come to our house for Thanksgiving. She makes a dish called three-cheese potatoes that is one of the best things I've ever tasted. It's why I really like Thanksgiving, even though the next day Mom and I always bring leftovers to my grandmother. She's in a nursing home. Mom actually visits Grandma every week, but she only makes me go with her once a month or so, and on special occasions, like Thanksgiving. It's really sad there. Once, Mom told me she hoped I would visit her often if she was ever in a home like that, and I got so upset because I didn't want to have to think about it: seeing Mom confused, sick, shriveled. It's true what they say about old people shrinking, because Grandma seems smaller every time I see her. She says the strangest things, too, which freaks me out sometimes.

"Leigh, I swear, don't worry about a thing," Vivette was saying. "I shouldn't have even said anything to you."

"No," Mom said. "This has gone on too long. Jonathan has no idea."

"You know this isn't the place to talk about this," Vivette said.

"You're the one who brought it up," Mom said. She sounded angry. Annie looked at me, but I just shrugged. We pushed our way through the rack of dresses. Mom had her hand pressed to her forehead. It was Vivette who noticed us first. "Hiya, Carly," she said. "Hi, Annie."

We said hi back, and right then Mom's whole face changed. She lowered her hand from her head and grinned. "Come on in, girls," she said, beckoning us. "I'm just about done for the day."

"Did you have fun today?" Vivette asked. She put her arm around my shoulder. When she does that—puts her arm around me, or gives me a hug—I feel like I'm being swallowed up. Vivette is really tall and broad. It's not that she's fat; actually, she's not fat at all, just muscular. Her shoulders are wide, like she's wearing shoulder pads, and she has thick wrists and ankles. My mom says Vivette is big-boned. I'm on the small side, like my mom. I've always been one of the shortest kids in my grade. Everyone says I have a gymnast's body, which is kind of funny just because I'm so completely inflexible. Anyway, I always feel like a really little kid when I stand next to Vivette.

"Yeah, of course," I said. "I love it here."

"Good, I'm glad," she said. "Listen, I have to get going. It was great to see you, girls . . . and Leigh, everything is under control." She kissed us all good-bye, and walked through the rack of clothes and out the door.

"What was that about?" I asked.

"What?"

"What you and Vivette were talking about?"

"Nothing," Mom said. She bent down to her desk and scribbled something on a piece of paper: *Violet in hotel dream sequence.* Then she taped it up onto a hanger behind her—a crimson-red dress was hanging from it. It had an incredibly low neckline. Sometimes they have to put body tape on the dresses so they stay in place and the actresses don't accidentally flash the crew while they're filming. Mom turned back to me. "It was absolutely nothing. Are you two ready to roll?"

"Sure," I said.

Mom pulled our coats out of the closet. "God, I can't believe the three-day weekend is almost officially over," Annie said. "I really don't want to go to school tomorrow. Most of it's like a waste of time anyway. It's not like I plan to be a historian or a scientist or anything like that, so why do I have to learn about those things?"

"I suppose you never know when they will come in handy," Mom said. "You could sound very intellectual at a dinner party."

"But you don't need them here, right, Leigh?" Annie asked. My friends all call Mom by her first name.

"I haven't yet," Mom said.

"And this is really what I want to do," Annie said. "I want to be an actress."

"Well, whatever you grow up to be, I had to learn about history and science, and your parents had to learn about history and science—so maybe we just want you guys to suffer like we did," Mom said. It was a Mom kind of thing to say—when people are upset, she tries to be funny and lighten the mood. "Come on, let's get out of here and grab some dinner."

We went to a Mexican restaurant not too far from the set, and afterward we got Mom's car out of the garage and headed back up to Westchester.

Annie and I both live in Westchester County, just in different towns. Annie lives in Scarsdale, and I live in New Rochelle. I don't have any friends from Preston who live near me. There's just Amelia, who lives across the street, but she goes to public school. When we were little, our mothers were really close. They're not as friendly as they used to be, since Mom's best friend is Vivette. Still, I like Amelia, and being friends with her is convenient. We can hang out without needing anyone to drive us anywhere. (Although Annie's parents have a driver, so generally it's not a problem. She can get dropped off at my house whenever she wants.)

In the car on the way home Annie and I sat in the backseat, like Mom was our chauffeur. Annie was talking about her parents, who are way different from mine. They're really stiff, and sort of unapproachable. In fact their whole house is stiff and unapproachable. They actually have rooms in it that we're not even allowed to go into, because the furniture is so special and expensive. But sometimes, when Annie's parents are out and Annie's busy in another room, I go into one of the forbidden rooms and look around. I run my fingers along the silk on the couch, and feel the wood on the antique dressers.

"My dad said he'll be late all week, so I know my mom will be in one of her annoying moods," Annie said.

I knew "annoying" wasn't really the right word for how Annie's mom would be. It was just code for how she'd be drinking. I've seen Annie's mother get drunk before—more than once. It usually happens when her dad is working late. Her mom sits at the dining room table with a bottle of wine and talks until her words are slurred.

Annie doesn't really talk about it. She's just got this weird thing with her mom: Sometimes she loves her and tries to be like her, glamorous and stuff, and sometimes she just hates her—mostly when she's drinking. I guess she can't really go up to her mom and say, "I don't think you should drink anymore." And she can't talk to her dad about it either. First of all he's not home that much, and second of all he's really intense and scary.

I just know, even though she doesn't say it, that it's easier for Annie when she stays at our house. Mom knows it too. "You can always stay with us if you want to," Mom told her.

"I wish I could," Annie said. "But my mom would never let me sleep over on a school night. She's got all these rules. It's so dumb."

I waited for Mom to say something to make Annie feel better, but all of a sudden there was a whooping sound and flashing lights behind us. Mom cursed under her breath and turned the knob on the car stereo. I hadn't even realized the music was on until then, when there was just silence.

"What's going on?" I asked.

"I don't know," Mom said. "I don't think I did anything wrong." There was something about the way her voice wavered that made me scared. We pulled to the side of the road. Mom pressed the button to roll down her window.

The officer leaned into the car. "Ma'am, are you aware you ran a stop sign at the bottom of the hill?"

"No, officer," Mom said. "I didn't see it."

"Can I have your license and registration please?"

"Of course, officer," Mom said. I watched from the backseat as she reached for her bag. She pulled her license out of her wallet. "I'm really sorry, officer. This is my license. The registration is the glove compartment—one sec." She leaned over, popped open the glove compartment, and handed the registration over to him.

"Thank you," the officer said.

"I just can't believe I did that. I was in the middle of a very intense conversation with these two—which is a terrible excuse. I was trying to be a role model, but I guess I'm not setting a good example for them after all. Girls, do as I say, not as I do."

The officer smiled. "Don't be too hard on yourself, Mrs. Wheeler," he said. "I'll tell you what—I'll let you go with a warning this time. Just watch the signs and drive carefully, all right?"

"Of course, officer," Mom said. "Thank you so much." We pulled away slowly. Mom took a deep breath and let it out slowly, like she was still nervous about the whole thing.

"That cop car is always there," Annie said. "He's always trying to catch people. Our driver got a ticket from him a few weeks ago. My mom says the cops probably give out more tickets at the end of the month, just so they can meet their quotas."

"But it's the twenty-seventh of the month now," I said.

"He must have been in a good mood," Mom said.

"Maybe," I said. "I think there's just something kind of magical about you," I said.

"Thanks, honey," she said. She smiled and sounded like herself again. "That's why your faux pa married me."

chapter two

Faux Pa is what I call my stepfather. My actual, biological father died when I was a baby. He was in a car accident on the Hutchinson River Parkway. One of Mom's friends had some leftover baby stuff that she was giving away, and my father drove up to get it—baby clothes, a playpen, and a fancy kind of stroller. On the way home the roads were slick with rain. The car in the lane next to his skidded into him. He spun around and got hit by oncoming traffic. Mom said someone rang the doorbell. She didn't hear it at first because she had a colicky baby—me—wailing in her arms. When she finally opened the door, there were two policemen on the front step. As soon as Mom saw them, she knew what had happened. She ran out of the house in her slippers and banged on our neighbors' door. Luckily the Sarsens—Amelia's parents—were home. Mrs. Sarsen was pregnant with Amelia at the time. She said she would take care of me, and Mr. Sarsen went with Mom to the hospital so she wouldn't have to be alone.

I know the whole story, but I don't remember my dad at all. I was six weeks old when he died, which I think sounds a lot more horrible than it actually is. I mean, I know it was really sad for my mom and my grandparents when it happened. But it's really hard to miss someone you don't even remember. There's a part of me that feels guilty about it, since obviously I was the whole reason Mom sent him to pick up the baby stuff in the first place. But the truth is that I don't even think about my dad that much anymore.

It's weird, because there are things about me that are because of him. I know from the photographs that I look sort of likc him. Mom has greenish eyes, but my dad had blue eyes, and so do I. Also, my name was his idea, and I'm thankful to him for that. I've always liked my name. I know most kids go through a phase when they don't. In fifth grade Annie hated her name so much that she started writing *A. Rebecca Rothschild* on top of anything she had to hand in for school. She said her stage name would be Rebecca Rothschild—she liked the double *R* sound, and she thought it sounded like the name of someone who should be famous. She told us all to call her Rebecca from then on, but it didn't really stick. Maybe one day I'll stop liking the name Carly, but so far it hasn't happened.

So this is how my dad came up with my name: On their first date my parents saw the singer Carly Simon in a restaurant. At least they thought it was her. The waiter refused to confirm it, and neither of them was bold enough to go over and ask for her autograph. But when they found out Mom was pregnant with a girl,

Dad said they should name the baby Carly. Now I wish they had gotten her autograph—I think it would be cool to have something signed by her.

Anyway, I'm lucky, because Faux Pa is a great father to me. Mom met him—Jonathan Wheeler—when I was six years old. They got married a year later. I was Mom's maid of honor. I was convinced that I was the youngest person to ever get to be a maid of honor, and I was really excited about it. I still have the dress I wore, in the back of my closet. It has pink fringe, kind of like a flapper dress. When I spun around on the dance floor, the fringe lifted up.

As soon as they were married, I wanted to call Jonathan Dad. But back then my real dad's parents were still alive, and Mom said it was very important to them that I not call anyone else Dad. So we tried to come up for a good name for Jonathan—something better than "stepfather," since that's more of a description than a name. Mom thought of Faux Pa. She and Jonathan thought it was hysterical, but I didn't get it, since I was only seven. Mom explained that *faux* is the French way of saying "fake." So he was my fake pa. But the funny part was that it was also a play on words: *faux pas* is an expression in French that means "mistake," and it's pronounced the exact same way. I don't think of Faux Pa as a mistake at all (and according to Ally's guru, there's no such thing), but the name stuck, and all of my parents' friends think it is very clever.

We have a good family. Faux Pa and Mom are really happy with each other. As far as I can tell, they are kind of proof of that whole "opposites attract" thing. Mom is really carefree and jokes a lot, and Faux Pa is more serious. She's very stylish (obviously, she has to be for her job). He's a physics professor, so it's not like clothing matters to him. It's perfectly normal for him to leave the house with mismatched socks on, or to wear a jacket that totally clashes with his shirt. Sometimes Mom gets on his case about it, but not in a mean way, just in a way that you know means she thinks it's sort of endearing. When they have an event to go to for anything related to *Lovelock Falls*, Mom always picks out his clothes.

Every other weekend Faux Pa's other kids visit us, the kids from his first marriage—Jessa, who is fourteen, and Justin, who is nine. Everyone in Faux Pa's old family has a *J* name: Jonathan, Jocelyn (that's his ex-wife), Jessa and Justin. My mom thinks it's really dumb. She likes that in our family we all have our own first initials—like we are individuals and can't share monogrammed shirts and towels. But actually, I think it would be nice to be connected like that. Our last name is Wheeler—my biological father's last name is now one of my middle names, so my full name is Carly Ruth Parker Wheeler. Sometimes I imagine changing Mom's and Faux Pa's first names to names that start with the letter *C*. I feel like it would prove we're meant to be a family.

It doesn't matter anyway, because most of the time Faux Pa seems more like my dad than Jessa and Justin's—I'm the kid he lives with full-time, so he ends up sharing more with me after all.

chapter three

Jessa and Justin were with us the next weekend. When they're around, Faux Pa sometimes does things with them, without Mom and me—I guess to make up for the fact that he doesn't see them as much. They go out for brunch, or to the bookstore, or to one of Justin's games. He plays hockey during the fall semester and baseball in the spring. Other times Faux Pa tries to think of activities for all of us to do together—trips into the city, to a museum or a show. In the winter, occasionally, we drive up to Vermont to go skiing. On regular weekends—the weekends when Jessa and Justin are with their mom—we don't usually go on any special field trips.

Generally, I like the weekends that I'm an only child better. I know that sounds bad, and I should say how much I love my stepsiblings, and how great it is to have them around. We get along fine; it's just sometimes I feel like I don't know them all that well.

Jessa is the kind of person who likes to do her own thing. Even when Faux Pa has one of his group activities planned, Jessa seems kind of distant. It's as if she's thinking about other things even when she's with you. She started high school this fall, and somehow she seems like more of a stranger. It's hard for me to have a conversation with her without feeling babyish, like she doesn't take me seriously. And Justin's a fourth-grade boy, so we don't have that much in common. He's really into video games and computer games, and basically anything electronic.

I also have to admit that it makes me feel weird when I hear Jessa and Justin call Faux Pa "Dad." Of course they do that—he is their dad, their *real* dad. Then I think about how to me he's just a *faux*: a fake. And it's not like we have such a big house—I mean, it's plenty big when there are just three of us, but when there are five of us, it feels a bit crowded. We don't have extra rooms the way Annie does—the Rothschilds have a bunch of spare bedrooms, but Jessa and Justin have to share a room in our house. I have my own room, which makes me feel a little guilty, because I know they hate sharing—Jessa especially. She's very organized and private about her stuff. I've heard her fighting with Justin, calling him a slob, and telling him to get out so she can talk on the phone without him listening in. That's another good thing about being an only child—I don't have anyone to fight with. It's not that I'm selfish; I'm just peaceful.

Anyway, it's nice to have Mom and Faux Pa to myself.

But then sometimes I wonder, what would I think about Jessa and Justin if we were born into the same family, as full siblings? If we lived together all the time?

Then they wouldn't have to see me as the girl who gets their dad all the time, and I wouldn't have to see them as the kids that maybe, just maybe, he loves more.

Faux Pa had decided that we would go bowling that night—Friday night. There's a bowling alley a few towns over from where we live. But Mom came home and said she'd had a really awful day at work. She had no energy for anything at all, so we ordered Chinese food instead. Usually Faux Pa doesn't like when we order in, because he thinks it's a waste of money, but I guess he felt bad for Mom, because he went to pick it up. He told Jessa and me to set the table while he was out—I think he likes it when she and I do things together. Jessa said we should set it up like a big buffet because it wouldn't take as long. She stacked the plates at the end of the table, and I wrapped napkins around the chopsticks.

When we were done, I went into the den to watch TV with Justin. Jessa picked up her book and settled into the chair in the corner of the room. Faux Pa came home a few minutes later. "Girls, I thought you were going to set the table."

"We did," Jessa said. "It's buffet style—like in Vegas."

"Is that so?" Faux Pa asked. "And when was the last time you were in Las Vegas, young lady?"

Jessa smiled slyly, without showing her teeth. I wondered if it was to hide her braces. She looks old for her age, I think because of the way she carries herself and because she's all filled out on top. You would think she was at least sixteen or seventeen years old, not fourteen, except if you saw she still had braces. "There's a lot you don't know about me, old man," she said. I had a feeling she was right about that. Her nostrils twitched, the way they sometimes do while she's talking. She happens to be really pretty. She has really dark hair—it would be wavy, except she blows it straight—and light blue eyes. Faux Pa says Jessa is the only one in his family with blue eyes, and that there must be a recessive gene buried in there. Everyone else's eyes are brown.

"I know you're still seven years away from being old enough to go there," he told her.

"It's not like there's a minimum age to visit Las Vegas," Jessa said. "You can go at any age, and I'm only about six and a half years away from being able to hang out in the casinos."

Faux Pa shook his head. "Don't remind me how old I'm getting."

"I wasn't talking about you; I was talking about me," Jessa said.

"Anyway, we thought it would be fun to eat like we're at a buffet, since we're all sharing everything anyway," I told him.

"I'm not sharing everything," Justin said. "I hate Chinese food, except for spare ribs."

"I know," Faux Pa said. "I got you your own order."

"Sweet," Justin said.

"Where's your mom, Carly?"

"Upstairs in your room, I think," I said.

"Go get her, will you? Tell her the food has arrived."

I ran to the bottom of the stairs and shouted upward: "Mo-om!" It's kind of a joke between Mom, Faux Pa, and me. He thinks Mom and I are really loud—like we talk at a higher-than-average decibel level. I turned back to him and grinned.

"You're funny, Carly," he said.

"I know," I said.

"I don't think she heard you," he said. "And don't shout again."

"Okay, I'll go upstairs." I sighed, as if it were going to be a really long journey.

Mom was sitting on her bed when I got to her room. She didn't see me come in. She was just there, looking at nothing. It was weird, because she's not the kind of person who usually sits and stares. She's always doing something—reading, watching TV, talking on the phone. Faux Pa is the one you catch sometimes just staring off into space. I guess maybe that's where Jessa gets it from.

"Mom?"

"Oh, hi, honey."

"Dinner's here."

"All right."

"Aren't you coming down?"

"I am," Mom said. "I'll be down in a minute."

"Are you okay?"

"Of course I am," Mom said. She held her hand out to me, and I took it and pulled, as if she needed help standing. "I like that shirt," she said.

I was wearing a short-sleeved sweater, nothing that fancy. It was turquoise and had a belt made of the same fabric, which looped around the middle. "Thanks," I said. "You got it for me."

"I remember," Mom said. "It looks great on you. You're all set clotheswise, right?"

"What do you mean?"

"There's nothing you need right now?"

I shrugged. "I'm still growing," I reminded her. "So I'm all set until I grow out of my jeans."

We headed downstairs. I grabbed a plate and loaded

up on fried rice and sesame chicken. The phone rang a few minutes later, and Mom got up to answer it. I was sort of surprised, because that's one of Faux Pa's rules—especially when Jessa and Justin are there, and we're eating as a family. He doesn't like anyone to talk on the phone. He says whoever's calling can leave a message, and we can talk to them when we're done with our meal.

"I'm sorry, Jon," Mom said. She picked up the receiver. "Hello?" There was a pause as Mom listened to whoever was on the other end. Then she turned back to Faux Pa. "Jon, I'm going to take this in the other room."

"So, Dad," Justin said, "you know how you were telling me about black holes?"

"I didn't know you were listening."

"I was, sort of," Justin said. "It was cool how the light gets swallowed up inside."

"It has to do with the gravitational pull," Faux Pa said.

"Uh-huh, well, you know how Jared and Eli and Ben and I can all play games on the computer at the same time, right?"

"I know," Faux Pa said.

"There's this super-cool new game called Black Hole Supernova," Justin said. "I think you'd like it. There's a team that's the black hole, and you try to conquer the supernova."

"That doesn't make sense," Faux Pa said.

"Mom hates it," Jessa said. "It's basically all he does now."

"She does not," Justin said. "It is not."

"She made a rule that he can only play a couple hours on the weekend."

"I just promised my friends that I'd play tonight,"

Justin said. "They're waiting on the computer for me. It's not right to just not show up."

"We were supposed to be bowling," Jessa said. "You wouldn't have played with them anyway."

"All right, Jess," Faux Pa said. "Let me be the parent."

"But you're not even around to know the rules," she said.

"You're lying about the rules," Justin said. "I heard Mom say she's worried about you because you're not social. At least I'm playing with my friends."

I looked at Faux Pa. This was something he never had to deal with where I was concerned. If Mom makes a rule for me, he knows about it. In fact, whatever the rules are, they usually come up with them together, like the one about me not getting a cell phone until I turn thirteen. I wondered if he would call Jocelyn, his ex-wife, to talk about what the rules should be for Justin using the computer. I hate thinking about him talking to Jocelyn. It's like he's cheating on Mom or something, even though I know it isn't really like that. Faux Pa says he tries to keep his relationship with Jocelyn "civil," for the sake of Jessa and Justin.

"Mom wouldn't say that," Jessa said. "I'm not the liar here."

"That's enough, you two," Faux Pa said.

"Can I use your computer, Dad, please?" Justin asked.

"When you're finished with dinner, yes, you can," Faux Pa said. "You can go on for thirty minutes."

"What if the game lasts longer? What if I need, like, forty-two minutes?"

"Forty minutes is the absolute limit," Faux Pa said. "Jessa's right—we were supposed to be bowling tonight, so that's a lot more time than you thought you'd have. Otherwise the deal is off."

"No, it's all right," Justin said. "It's a deal."

"Good, and after that we'll do something all together. We'll play Monopoly or something."

"Mom's not going to be happy about this," Jessa said.

"Don't worry about it," Faux Pa said. "Let's change the subject. Tell me about school."

Jessa shrugged. "There's nothing to tell."

"Is geometry any better?"

"Not really," Jessa said. "Miss Margolis is a jerk."

"Jon?" Mom called from the top of the stairs. "Can you come here a minute?"

I looked at Faux Pa and smiled, waiting for him to say something about Mom's decibel level, and how she should've just come downstairs herself if she had something to tell him. But before he could say anything, Mom called out again. "Jon, it's important!"

Faux Pa stood up. "What's going on?" I asked.

"I'm sure everything is fine, Carly," he said. "Don't worry."

He headed upstairs. Justin went to play on Faux Pa's computer. Jessa brought her plate into the kitchen and then headed back to the den to read. The leftover food was still on the table. I knew it wasn't really my job to clean it all up, but I started closing the containers. I put the leftover chicken in the fridge.

Justin wandered into the kitchen. "Do you know the password for my dad's computer?"

"I think it's 'Clifton Court,'" I said. That was the name of the street Faux Pa grew up on. "But smushed together so it's all one word."

"I tried that, but it didn't work," Justin said.

"Maybe he changed it," I said. He changes it every so often. "Go upstairs and ask him."

Justin left the room and came back a couple minutes later. "Their door was closed," he reported.

"Did you knock?" I asked.

"No, can you just go get him?"

I could tell Justin didn't want to knock, because he's shy around my mom. There really isn't any reason for him to be like that. After all, he's known my mother most of his life. But I guess if you're only seeing someone every other weekend, you never feel completely related to her. "Sure," I said.

I went upstairs. When I was younger, I used to just barge into Mom and Faux Pa's room when their door was closed. Now I worry about what they may be doing inside. I don't want to see anything gross. So I raised my hand to knock. I could hear their voices on the other side, and I stopped. "I don't want you to get involved in this," Faux Pa said.

"You don't understand, Jon," Mom said.

"What? What don't I understand? Is there something you're not telling me?"

"No," Mom said.

"I know she's your friend, Leigh, but really. Maybe you should talk to an attorney before you speak to her again, just to check the legal ramifications. You don't want to get mixed up in this, believe me. Eric's a lawyer—I can give him a call, and he can tell you." Eric is one of Mom and Faux Pa's friends. He works with Faux Pa at the university, as a professor in the history department. I didn't know he was a lawyer, too.

"He's not a practicing lawyer," Mom said.

"Well, then I'm sure he knows someone," Faux Pa

said. "He must have friends from law school."

I remembered the conversation I'd overheard in Mom's office, when she was talking to Vivette. I was overhearing a lot lately. It made me feel like a spy—like I was doing something wrong. Behind the door Faux Pa said "sugar," which is his curse word, the word he trained himself to use so he wouldn't say anything offensive in front of us kids. I think it's funny, because of course we know those other words. Even Justin knows them.

Standing at the door right then, part of me wanted to walk away. But they were talking about lawyers, and I wanted to know why. I turned the knob and pushed open the door. "What's going on?" I asked.

"Nothing," Mom said, just like she'd said when I'd asked her about her conversation with Vivette.

"I heard you guys talking just now," I said, feeling guilty. "Why do you need a lawyer?"

"I don't," Mom said.

"Leigh," Faux Pa said.

"Really, Jonathan."

"So what were you talking about?" I asked.

"Nothing," Mom said again.

"This is going to get out, Leigh," Faux Pa said. "She's going to find out. It may as well be now—it may as well be from you, instead of something she reads in a magazine. You know how public these things can be."

I felt myself getting scared—palms starting to sweat, heart beating faster. "What?" I asked.

Mom sighed. "Vivette was arrested today," she said.

chapter four

Vivette was accused of using her corporate credit card—the card *Lovelock Falls* gave her to buy clothing for the show—to buy things for herself. It got out, like Faux Pa said. There were stories in the newspaper about how someone who worked at *Lovelock Falls* had been arrested for stealing. "Embezzlement," the papers called it. They said Vivette had racked up thousands of dollars of charges, and the police were still investigating to see how much money she'd spent.

I didn't want to bother Mom, because she was so upset about the whole thing. I knew I would feel awful if Annie got in trouble for cheating, or anything like that. Faux Pa said Mom didn't have anything to do with it, except everyone at *Lovelock Falls* was going to be interviewed to see what they knew. Mom was at the top of the list, since she was Vivette's best friend and they worked in the same department. Faux Pa made Mom speak to his friend Eric first. He's really cautious about things like that.

In the meantime Vivette wasn't in jail anymore; she was out on bail.

Out on bail. It sounded like something in a movie. Because of the newspaper articles, everyone at school had heard about it. "I can't believe we just saw that woman," Annie said. "I've never known anyone who was arrested before."

Talking about Vivette did a funny thing to my stomach. Vivette, who made the best potatoes, who told me I was like the daughter she never had. Mom once told me that Vivette couldn't have children of her own. I put down the slice of pizza I was holding without taking a bite. "Me either," I said.

It was Tuesday—four days after Vivette was arrested—and we were having lunch at Slice of Life, the pizza place down the block from school. Annie and I were on one side of a booth, and our friends Lauren and Jordan were on the other side. We were lucky to get a booth, since the place totally fills up with kids from our school, but Annie has fourth period free on Tuesdays, so she always runs over to get us seats.

Mom is actually the whole reason we were allowed off campus during lunch. The rule at Preston is that, starting in seventh grade, students don't have to have lunch in the cafeteria. It's not that there are so many options off campus—you need a car to go anywhere good, which obviously my friends and I don't have. But it's just more fun to be able to get away from school in the middle of the day. There's a strip mall in walking distance, where Slice of Life is, along with a deli, and there's also a diner around the corner.

But in September these two eighth graders, Michelle Nelson and Carrie Lincoln, left school at lunch and went back to Carrie's house. Her parents weren't home, and they raided the liquor cabinet, got drunk, and skipped the rest of the day of school. I'm not exactly sure how the Preston Day School administration found out, though there are a lot of rumors about who told on them. It was a big scandal, and they were suspended for a week. Then the Parents' Council had a meeting with the school administration about it—the Parents' Council is the name of the group of parents that get involved in school things. My mom is a part of it, even though she says a lot of the other members are really conservative and stuck-up. They were all fired up about what Michelle and Carrie did, and everyone decided that students shouldn't be allowed off campus during lunch anymore. Mom stood up and said that wasn't fair. She said they were blowing things out of proportion, and that the rest of us shouldn't be deemed untrustworthy and punished just because of the actions of two kids. Then, as Mom said, cooler heads prevailed—they decided we could go off campus for lunch, but that if there was ever another incident, the privilege would be revoked for everyone.

"So are you going to talk to Ally about Vivette this weekend?" Annie asked.

"What?" I asked.

"Aren't you seeing her on Saturday when you babysit?"

"Oh, yeah," I said. "I'm supposed to. I have to ask my mom if we're still going."

"Why wouldn't you?"

"I probably am," I said. "It's just that my mom's really upset."

"Did Vivette say for sure that she did it?" Jordan asked. Jordan likes to get the details on everything, even about people she doesn't know.

"I don't know," I said. "My mom hasn't talked to her."

Vivette had called our house a couple of times, but Faux Pa wouldn't let Mom take her calls. I knew that was one of the hardest things for Mom. Every time Vivette called and Faux Pa said Mom couldn't come to the phone, Mom looked like she was in actual physical pain. But Eric had said that any conversation Mom had with Vivette would be something the police would question her about.

"But don't you think your mom knew what Vivette was doing?" Annie asked.

I shook my head, even though I was sure Mom really had known. We'd heard her tell Vivette: *This has gone on too long. Jonathan has no idea.* It just kept running through my head. Faux Pa didn't want Mom to get mixed up in it, but she already was. What did it matter, anyway? It wasn't like Mom could be arrested for something Vivette had done; at least I didn't think so.

"You know, she's innocent until proven guilty," Lauren said. For a second I thought she was talking about my mom.

"Come on," Annie said, "she was arrested. She had to have been doing something wrong. People don't just get arrested out of the blue."

I hated to admit it, but I agreed with her.

"Hey, you guys," Annie said, her voice suddenly a whisper, "Alex Jedder just walked in."

Alex is in our grade, and he's the cutest guy in school; everyone agrees on that. He also happens to be my science lab partner. Annie was totally jealous about that at first. She said she couldn't believe I got to spend fifty minutes with him each day. I told her she didn't have anything to worry about; we were just lab partners, and that was it. Besides, it's not like I picked Alex to be my partner. Our teacher, Dr. Sherman, randomly assigned us our lab partners on the first day of class.

I'm good in science. Maybe from living with Faux Pa for so many years, the science stuff rubbed off on me. Last year I got an honorable mention for my experiment about seed germination, and Alex doesn't mind using the Bunsen burner, which I hate, so we're a good pair.

"Oh, God, his smile," Annie was saying, "it could melt butter. Even butter that's been in the freezer for a really long time—he could just melt it."

"Totally," Jordan agreed.

"What do you think he was doing for the last twenty minutes?" Annie asked. "Lunch is already half over. There aren't even any seats left in here."

It was true—Slice of Life was crowded with Preston kids. I bet if the decision to not let us off campus during lunch had stuck, the place would've gone out of business.

"Maybe he had to stay after class for something," I said.

"Maybe he was on the phone," Jordan said.

"Or maybe he was in the bathroom," Lauren said, smiling.

Alex jammed himself into the booth across from us, which already had four people in it, next to this kid Trevor Christopher, who's in my English class. He's probably the second cutest guy in our grade. The cute guys always hang out together, like it's a special club.

Annie turned to me. "I can't decide if you should ask

him if he likes me," she said. "Is that too weird? I mean, would he think that's weird?"

"I don't know," I said. "I don't know what he thinks."

"I wish he would just ask you about me himself!"

"Yeah, me too," I said. The thing was, Alex and I had sort of become friends. Not the kind of friends who hang out after school or on the weekends, but friends the way you are when you're in class with someone and you like talking to them. I hadn't told Annie about it, because I knew she would think it was a big deal that I was getting to be friends with Alex Jedder. It wasn't like we were dating, or even close to it. I didn't think of him that way, really. But now there was this thing—this secret—that I was keeping from my best friend. For some reason I started thinking about Mom and Vivette again. Mom never really kept secrets from me, and she definitely wouldn't keep anything from Faux Pa . . . except she'd said, *Jonathan has no idea.* It made sense if she was keeping a secret for Vivette. I guess I would do the same thing for one of my friends.

"Stop staring at him," Annie said. "He'll know we're talking about him."

I was in a total daydream, and I hadn't realized I was still looking at Alex. I snapped my head back. "Sorry," I said.

"Oh my God, did he just wink at you?" Annie asked.

"I don't know," I said. "You told me not to look over there."

"I swear he did," she said. She sounded mad. No, not mad exactly, but definitely upset.

"He must have had something in his eye," I said. "I doubt that he really winked. Why would he do that?"

"If you like him, it's fine," Annie said, in a way that I

knew it really wasn't. "You should just tell me."

"I don't," I said. "I mean, not that way. We're just partners in science class."

That seemed to make sense to Annie, for whatever reason. I could see her relaxing about the whole thing. "Hey, remember how when we were little, we invited all the boys to our birthday parties, but then boys started to be uncool, so we stopped inviting them?"

I nodded. "Yeah," Lauren said. "Because we decided they were gross and had cooties."

"Exactly," Annie said, laughing. "But they're slightly less gross now. So I'm going to invite boys to my birthday party again this year. I just decided. What do you think?" It didn't surprise me that Annie was talking about her birthday over two months before the actual date—she always feels a lot of pressure to do something great, since it falls right around Christmas. She doesn't want people to get swept up in holiday stuff and forget about her birthday.

"I think that sounds good," Jordan said. "Will you invite, like, the same number of boys as there are girls, so it all matches up?"

"I don't know," Annie said. "I still have to work out the details. Obviously, you guys are all invited."

"Obviously," Jordan said. "Who else?"

Annie started to make a list of familiar names—mostly the popular kids in our grade—the four of us, and then other girls like Elana Bronstein, Ellie Oxberg, and Lily O'Mara. After that came the popular boys.

I guess we're lucky to be popular. I don't mean that to sound obnoxious—the biggest reason that I'm popular is that I'm Annie Rothschild's best friend. It's not even that I care so much about popularity, and I honestly try to be nice to everyone. It just definitely makes things easier when everyone thinks you're cool. You don't get picked last for things, and people come to your birthday parties. I know it would be harder to be someone like Ginny Winkler. She's this girl in our grade who talks to herself sometimes. If something pops into her head, she just says it out loud. There's nothing really wrong with her. She's kind of chubby and a little weird, but she's perfectly nice. It wasn't fair that she wasn't on Annie's list, but it's just the way these things are.

The lunch period was almost over, so we had to head back to school. We threw away our paper plates and napkins. Some kids leave their garbage on the table, which I think is completely rude.

Outside, it was raining—not a lot, just a little drizzle. I hadn't known it was going to rain, and I really hate how frizzy my hair gets. Annie produced an umbrella from her book bag. She grabbed my arm and pulled me underneath it. "What are you doing after school?"

"Nothing much," I said. "We have that history quiz tomorrow."

The seventh-grade curriculum is American Government & Law—which is kind of a weird history class. We learn about some old Supreme Court cases, but mostly we learn about how the government is set up. So it's not exactly history as much as how things work in the present. "Oh, right," Annie said. "Can I come over to study?"

"Don't you have tennis today?"

"Scott called last night and said he has the flu," she said. Scott is the name of her tennis instructor.

"Sure, come over," I said.

"Hey, look at that," Lauren said suddenly. She was up ahead of us. She didn't have an umbrella, but her hair is always stick straight, no matter what the weather is. She's Asian—Korean, actually—and she says hair like that is her birthright.

Annie and I stopped to look where Lauren was pointing. There, up above the hills, was a rainbow. I hadn't seen a rainbow in a long time. I love them. "Oh, wow," I said.

The colors were really bright. It made the sky so pretty, even though everything else was gray. I remembered that rainbows were supposed to be lucky—something about leprechauns and the pot of gold at the other end. For some reason Ally's guru popped into my head. I decided the rainbow was a sign that everything would work out. I'd get an A on the history quiz, and Annie would have a great party, and all the crazy stuff with Vivette being arrested and that weird conversation with Mom—all of that would be just fine.

chapter five

Annie and I like to make up commercials sometimes. I know that sounds kind of dumb, but it's really fun. It started out that we would just imitate the commercials we saw on TV, but now we make ones up for things we think should exist. Our favorite made-up product is a pill we call the Visibility Zapper, which makes you suddenly invisible to teachers. It would be especially helpful to take right before American Government & Law, since our teacher, Mrs. Harrity, likes to call on kids even if they aren't raising their hands. She'll just pick someone at random—it's called the Socratic Method—and then fire question after question. I think she actually likes it when the student she calls on doesn't know the answer. She gets this evil smile on her face whenever she figures out that someone didn't do the reading from the night before.

Actually, that was the whole reason we were being

given a quiz on Wednesday. Ethan Rater couldn't explain the concept of separation of powers, so Mrs. Harrity said we'd all be tested on our knowledge of the legislative, judicial, and executive branches of government. Then she smiled her evil smile.

That afternoon the Rothschilds' driver dropped Annie and me off in front of my house. Usually Faux Pa drives me to school, since otherwise I would have to wake up an hour earlier just to catch the bus, but I take the bus home, so it was really nice to have a chauffeur. We got out of the car, and he drove off to run errands for Mrs. Rothschild. Mom was watching television in the den when Annie and I walked in. She stood up when she saw us. "Hi, girls."

"Hey," I said. "What are you doing home?"

"Production wrapped early."

"You didn't have to do any shopping for the show?" I asked. That was a big part of Mom's job—when they weren't filming, she would go to all the best stores in New York. They would have clothing all picked out in the right sizes, just waiting for Mom to come in and decide what would be good for the characters to wear.

Mom shook her head. "I didn't sleep that well last night, so I just came home."

"Are you okay?" I asked. I knew the mess had to do with Vivette, and I was worried all over again about Mom getting into trouble over what Vivette did.

"I'm fine," Mom said. She smiled, though I could tell it was kind of forced. "Do you two need anything?"

"We're good," I said. "Actually, we have a history quiz, so we're just going to hang out and study."

"I'll be up in my room if you need anything," Mom said.

I went into the kitchen to get sodas for Annie and me. When I got back, Annie was standing in the center of the room, holding our history textbook under her arm. "Do you have trouble studying?" she asked, in her mock announcer's voice. "Do you think it's mind-numbingly boring to memorize facts about things that happened to people you don't even know, and actually pointless, since you'll never need the information again anyway? Well, we have just the thing for you."

I put our drinks down on the coffee table and jumped right in. "That's right," I said. "Just take this special vitamin supplement. It's called Study No More, and you'll be able to memorize loads of information in just seconds."

"The way it works," Annie explained, "you just put your textbook in an ordinary kitchen blender, throw in two tablespoons of the Study No More powder, mix it all together, and then drink it up."

"Our patented formula comes in scrumptious flavors like bubble gum and cherry pie," I said.

"Or my personal favorite, cookie-dough boysenberry banana-split sundae," Annie said. "But don't wait too long to call—if you buy now, we will double your order."

"And all you have to pay is the shipping and handling," I added.

We looked at each other and started cracking up. Some of the most fun times I've ever had have been with Annie.

Annie tossed her textbook onto the couch. "I am *so* not in the mood to study," she said. "What is it again? Chapter seven?"

"Seven and eight," I said.

"Ugh," Annie said, sinking into the couch. "How

about if we plan my party first, and then study?"

"Okay," I said, "but we should put a time limit on it—like we can party-plan for a half hour, but then we really need to study."

Annie made a face. "God, I hate Mrs. Harrity."

"I know," I said.

"All right, a half hour," she said. "So this is what I'm thinking—if I'm going to have boys at this party, it can't just be a bunch of us hanging out at my house eating pizza, right?"

"I guess not," I said.

"Would it be really dumb to have a theme for my party, or really fun? I mean, it's my thirteenth birthday, so I don't want to seem like a baby."

Annie is the oldest of all of us—she was going to be a teenager months before any of the rest of us. I think she felt like she had a certain responsibility to be sophisticated. "People have themes for their sweet-sixteen parties," I reminded her. "It isn't babyish. Remember Elana was talking about her sister's fiesta party a couple weeks ago? They had it at a Mexican restaurant, and everyone ate fajitas, and they handed out maracas."

"Yeah, I guess a theme could be cool," Annie said.

"You could do some sort of rock and roll party," I suggested. "Like that restaurant in White Plains with all the jukeboxes that play music from the fifties and sixties."

"Maybe," Annie said. "But the thing is, I want to have more modern music, not that old-fashioned stuff."

"Yeah." I paused for a few seconds, thinking. "How about a casino—like Las Vegas?" I said, remembering Jessa.

"Monte Carlo would be even cooler," Annie said.

"What's Monte Carlo?"

"It's this place in Europe where they have parties and gambling," she said. "Really rich and famous people go there."

"Oh, wait," I said. "I've got it—a movie-star theme."

"That's perfect for me," Annie said. "We could have a red carpet. It could be like an awards show."

"But then it's like a really fancy party," I said.

"So?" Annie said. "You have that blue dress you never wear."

"I haven't had anything to wear it to yet," I said.

"Well, this would be perfect," Annie said. "And maybe your mom could even hook me up with something from thc *Lovelock Falls* wardrobe." Mom had done that for Annie and me once before, when we had to get dressed up for a cocktail party Annie's parents were having.

"I'll ask her," I said. I knew it would be fun to have an excuse to get all dressed up. "Do you think the boys will mind having to wear suits?"

"If the party is cool enough, they won't mind," Annie said. "I just hope Alex can come. Will you mention it in science? You don't have to say I told you to tell him. Just sort of casually say that it's going to be the party of the year."

"Do you think your parents will be into this?"

"Into what?"

"Letting you have a really big party?"

"Are you kidding? My mom loves planning parties. So will you tell Alex?"

"Sure," I said. "Don't worry."

It seemed strange to be planning a huge party just

to get Alex Jedder to like Annie, but I had to admit that it sounded fun. Annie took a sip of her Sprite. "I think we should have movie posters on the walls," she said. "We just have to figure out which ones to get."

She pulled out a piece of paper, and we sat down on the couch. We were debating whether we should have posters of new movies, or old movies that had already won awards. Then the doorbell rang. "It's probably Amelia," I said.

Sometimes Amelia comes over after school. The main reason we're friends is that we live so close to each other. Hanging out with her is so different from being with Annie. I once heard Jessa say that every friendship has a superhero and a sidekick. With Annie I am definitely the sidekick, but with Amelia I'm the superhero.

I really like Amelia a lot. I've known her since we were little. We used to make up recipes together, to try and create the world's most perfect cookie. But it's hard sometimes, because she doesn't go to Preston, so we don't have the same schedule or know any of the same people. Annie didn't know her well enough to invite her to her birthday party, so it would kind of be awkward for her to hang out with us. She's really sensitive, too. In fourth grade she cried at my birthday party because she wasn't one of the first people picked for teams when we were having a hula-hoop contest, even though it was just because she went to a different school and people didn't really know her that well. But I figured I would just tell her we were studying for our history quiz—which was sort of the truth. Our thirty minutes of party planning was almost up.

I got to the door and opened it without asking who

it was first, which was something Mom and Faux Pa would've been mad about. I was just so sure it was Amelia, but when I swung open the door, there were two people standing there—a man and a woman—looking very serious and official. "Is your mother home?" the man asked. He was in a uniform, and so was the woman. Navy blue pants and shirts with the letters *FBI* stitched in yellow. My stomach felt like it suddenly turned over. Something awful was happening; after all, the FBI doesn't just drop by for no reason. Mom said it was the police who came to the door when my real dad died, but maybe the FBI made house calls too. Maybe Faux Pa had been in an accident. I tried to remember his Tuesday school schedule. I had his whole schedule memorized, but my mind suddenly didn't work right.

I was just standing there, stupidly. The man flashed his badge. "I'm Special Agent Dixon Smith. This is Special Agent Marisa Valdez. We really need to speak to your mother."

"Okay," I said.

Years ago, Mom had told me that if strangers ever came to the door, I was to keep the door closed and make them wait outside. But I didn't close the door. I just ran to the stairs and shouted for Mom.

She came downstairs. The woman, Special Agent Marisa Valdez, asked to speak to her outside. I clenched my fists and thought to myself, quickly, *Please let Faux Pa be okay.* "I can't," Mom said to the agent. She turned to me. "My daughter is here."

"I don't want to make this more difficult," Special Agent Valdez said.

"Please," Mom said. "My husband will be home in

an hour." *Faux Pa will be home*, I thought. *He's okay. Everything will be okay*.

Special Agent Dixon Smith took a step forward, closer. "Leigh Catherine Wheeler, you are under arrest," he said. "You have the right to remain silent. Anything you say can and will be used against you in a court of law. You have the right to have a lawyer present during questioning. If you cannot afford a lawyer, one will be appointed for you."

And then, just like that, he brought out a pair of handcuffs. I knew it meant that Faux Pa was alive and well, but the whole thing was crazy. It was just like on TV, except it was real life—my life—happening right there. Right in our front hallway, my mom was being handcuffed. Her hands were behind her back. I heard a click when the cuffs were locked into place. I couldn't believe it.

"Mrs. Wheeler, do you understand these rights?" Special Agent Smith asked.

"Yes," Mom said.

"No," I said. Tears sprang to my eyes, and Annie clutched me. I had forgotten about her, but there she was—at my side. I grabbed her hand back. I knew this had to do with Vivette, and there was so much I wanted to say. It was Vivette's fault, not Mom's. Vivette had done it. Mom hadn't told on her because she was trying to protect her friend, but she'd tried to get Vivette to stop—she'd told her it had gone on too long. But then I remembered the right to remain silent—did that mean I wasn't allowed to speak either?

I looked at Special Agent Marisa Valdez. She wasn't the one who had read my mother her rights and put her in handcuffs. She was a woman, and for some reason I thought maybe she would be nice and understand that this shouldn't be happening. But her face didn't soften at all when she saw me looking at her. She was really cruel-looking. I noticed she was wearing a wedding ring. I bet her husband was really awful. If she had kids, then I felt sorry for them. "We'll have to take you girls with us to the federal marshal's office until someone, the next of kin, can pick you up," she said.

"Oh, God," Mom said, even though she wasn't supposed to talk.

"Come on, girls," Special Agent Valdez said.

"I don't even live here," Annie said.

"You still need to come in," the agent said.

"But she isn't my mother," Annie said. "If I call my mom now, she'll send our driver over to come get me. I'm sure he'll pick up Carly, too."

Special Agent Valdez raised an eyebrow when Annie said "our driver." I wished she hadn't said that. "We'll call your mom when we get to the office," the agent said.

chapter six

We didn't really talk in the car. The agents were in the front seat. Special Agent Smith was driving, and I was in between Mom and Annie in the backseat. It was so awful, because Mom was handcuffed, her hands behind her back. She had to sit forward a little bit, and it seemed really uncomfortable. She was crying, but she couldn't wipe her eyes. She couldn't even put on her seat belt. It seemed so strange that the FBI would make it so Mom couldn't wear a seat belt. It was against the law, and they were supposed to be upholding the law.

Annie was holding my hand. *We were just planning a party,* I thought to myself. *We're supposed to be studying for our history quiz.*

When we got there, Special Agent Smith took Mom into a back room and told Annie and me to sit on a bench. I knew it was stupid, but my heart was pounding, because I was worried I'd never see my mom again.

I felt raw, like she'd been ripped away from me. Part of me was glad Annie was there, next to me, so I didn't have to be alone, but another part of me just wished nobody were there to see. Now everyone at school would know about this.

Special Agent Valdez, who I had started calling Cruella in my head, asked us for the phone numbers of Annie's mom and Faux Pa's office. Annie's mom was the first to arrive. When Mrs. Rothschild walked in, Annie and I both jumped up. "Darlings," she said, kissing us hello. She was dressed the way she always is—sort of formal, even though she doesn't go to work during the day: slacks, a crisp shirt, a cable-knit sweater over her shoulders, and a silk scarf tied around her neck. She looked out of place at the station. Everything around us was so worn and gray, but Mrs. Rothschild looked clean and fresh. "I'm sorry I took so long. I had to wait for Gerry to come back with the car and pick me up. What's going on?"

I shrugged. If I started talking about it, I might cry again.

"This place is dreadful," Mrs. Rothschild said. "I'm going to go speak to someone." Her shoes clicked as she walked across the floor toward the front desk, as if she were wearing tap shoes. A couple minutes later she came back. "All right, Annie, we can go," she said.

"Can Carly come home with us?" Annie asked.

"The agent said she called her stepfather, so I'm sure he'll be here soon," Mrs. Rothschild said.

I swallowed hard. "I hope so," I said.

"Hang in there, darling," Mrs. Rothschild said, rubbing my arm quickly. She kissed my cheek again and pulled her keys out of her purse.

Annie kissed me too, an air kiss, which isn't how we usually say good-bye, but when Annie is in front of her mom, she acts a little different. And I guess there was nothing usual about us sitting there on a bench at the federal marshal's office, with Mom in a pair of handcuffs somewhere in the back. "Call me later, okay?" Annie asked.

"Okay," I said.

My mom wouldn't have ever left Annie alone in the FBI station, and I was sort of surprised that Mrs. Rothschild hadn't let me go home with them, or at least offered to stay with me until Faux Pa got there. But Mrs. Rothschild and my mom are such different people, and it's not like I even wanted to go; I wanted to find out what was happening to Mom first.

Faux Pa came in a few minutes later. I stood up from the bench. He grabbed me, and I started sobbing. He held me tight, rubbing my back, up and down, up and down. Special Agent Valdez came out, but I didn't pay any attention to her. "Mr. Wheeler," she said.

"Yes," Faux Pa said, releasing me a little bit.

"I'll need you to sign some paperwork, and then you can take your daughter home," she said.

"Where's my wife?" Faux Pa asked. I noticed a spot on his shirt that was a darker shade of green than the rest of it, wet from my tears.

"She's being held," Agent Valdez said. "She's asked for her attorney before we question her."

"Can I see her?"

"I'm afraid not."

"I really need to see my wife," Faux Pa said.

"She'll likely be arraigned in the morning," Agent Valdez said. "I'm sure her attorney will brief you."

"She won't be released after questioning?"

"Mr. Wheeler, there are some serious crimes at issue here."

"Like what?" Faux Pa asked.

"Conspiracy and embezzlement." I already knew what embezzlement was, and I was pretty sure conspiracy meant the FBI knew Vivette had told Mom what she was doing. It was all Vivette's fault.

Faux Pa shook his head. "This is crazy," he said. "This is ludicrous."

"Mr. Wheeler," Agent Valdez said, "there's paperwork."

"What about bail?" Faux Pa asked.

"At this point it won't be set until tomorrow."

"Does that mean Mom has to stay here, like in jail?" I asked.

I was talking to Faux Pa, but Agent Valdez, aka Cruella, answered. "Yes," she said.

It was all so wrong. Vivette did something awful, and it was being taken out on Mom. I remembered how Mom had stood up at the Preston parents' meeting after Michelle Nelson and Carrie Lincoln got caught. She said the other students shouldn't be punished for the actions of two kids. Now she was being punished because of Vivette's actions. "But this isn't right," I said. "She wasn't the one who did all those things. It was Vivette, so why should my mom have to be in jail? I need her to come home." Vivette didn't have kids, so it wouldn't even matter as much if she were in jail.

"Carly, honey, don't worry," Faux Pa said. "Just sit here for a few minutes so I can speak to the agent, okay?" He glared at Agent Valdez. "This is a misunderstanding. It will all get worked out."

I sat down while Faux Pa walked away with Cruella.

They were talking too softly for me to hear, but I could see them, and I watched her. She was sort of like a statue, the way there wasn't any expression to her face. It was like she was made of stone and didn't have any sympathy for people.

Faux Pa came back over to me. "Let's go, baby," he said. "I'm going to call the lawyer and figure this all out. Mom will be home tomorrow at the latest. Let me get you home, okay?"

I stood up and took his hand and walked with him out to the car, leaving Mom alone in that horrible building.

chapter seven

I couldn't believe Mom had to spend the night in jail. My mom, in jail. In my head I could see her in a cell with a bunch of other women, all of them dressed in those special clothes that sort of look like pajamas: boxy button-down shirts in some tacky color, like orange or bright blue, and matching pants. Did they talk to each other? What happened when one of them had to go to the bathroom? Did they sleep? I imagined the cell was very cold. I could never fall asleep unless I was under a blanket, cozy and warm. So were they all there, awake together all night long? I was so worried for Mom, because of the kinds of people she might be with, like murderers and drug dealers. She didn't belong there at all.

In the morning there was a knock on my door. I knew it had to be Faux Pa, because Mom was in jail. "Come in," I said.

I watched the knob twist, and then there was Faux Pa in the doorway, dressed up like he was going to work—khaki pants and a navy blazer. Under the blazer he had a white button-down shirt with a sort of boxed pattern on it, like the shirt was made of graph paper. It wasn't really stylish, but it was a good shirt for a teacher or a scientist, not that Faux Pa would have even thought of that when he picked it out. I glanced down at his feet—black loafers instead of brown. "Your shoes don't match," I said. "They should be brown so they don't clash with the navy blazer."

"I guess you're right," he said. "I'll change them before I go. Were you able to sleep at all?"

I shook my head. "Not really."

"I spoke to the lawyer, and the arraignment's set for this morning—ten o'clock."

"I don't even really understand what an arraignment is," I said.

"It's when a defendant first appears before a judge and has to plead guilty or not guilty."

I swallowed hard. "That sounds so serious," I said.

"It's just a formality," Faux Pa said.

"So Mom will tell the judge she's not guilty, and the judge will believe her and let her come home?"

"I don't know if the judge will believe her," Faux Pa said. "But she'll plead not guilty, and bail will be set—that's how they make sure a defendant won't leave town while awaiting trial. Once we pay it, she'll get to come home." He paused. "What a mess this is." He sounded angry, all of a sudden.

"It's not Mom's fault," I reminded him. "Vivette did it." It was funny how quickly I'd stopped liking Vivette. I'd known her for so many years, and now I didn't even care about what happened to her. "Just because Mom knew what Vivette was doing doesn't mean she should be punished too!"

"Did your mom tell you she knew what Vivette was doing?"

"Not exactly," I said. "I heard them talking once."

"What did they say?" I didn't answer right away. Faux Pa was looking at me sternly. "Carly, this is important."

"Mom said, 'This has gone on too long.' "

"When?"

"When Annie and I went to the set with Mom," I told him. "Vivette was talking to Mom in their office. They didn't see us come in."

"Annie was there too?"

"Yeah," I said.

Faux Pa shook his head. "Sugar," he said.

"What?" I asked. "Could Annie and I be in trouble too, just because we heard them talking?"

"No, baby, of course not," Faux Pa said. "Let's just keep this between you and me for now. Don't worry about it. Don't worry about a thing. I'm going to head over to meet Dale."

"Is Dale the lawyer?" I asked.

"Yes," Faux Pa said. "Why don't you lie down and try and get some sleep. You look about as exhausted as I feel."

I was relieved that he wasn't going to try and make me go to school, but then I thought that if there wasn't anything to worry about, he probably would expect me to go. "Can I go to the arraignment with you?"

"No, just stay here. I'll call you as soon as I know anything."

"But maybe the judge would be nicer to Mom if she saw me—if she saw Mom had a kid."

"It's not like that," Faux Pa said. "She's not on trial right now. She's not being sentenced. There shouldn't be any problem getting her released on bail today."

"Okay," I said.

"Are you all right staying here alone? Do you want me to see if I can find someone to stay with you?"

"No, it's okay," I said. "Just promise you'll bring Mom back home with you."

"I will," Faux Pa said.

He left a few minutes later. I pulled the covers up around me, but it was impossible to fall asleep. Even though my bed was warm and cozy, I couldn't get relaxed enough. I kept thinking about Mom in jail. I pictured one of the guards calling to her—"Leigh Wheeler, time for you to go." And Mom standing up, putting her wrists behind her back to be handcuffed again, and riding in the back of a car to the courthouse.

I'd never been in a courtroom. The one I pictured in my head was the one from *Lovelock Falls*. There had been a whole storyline on the show a few months earlier. One of the characters, Jazz Gallagher, was on trial for kidnapping someone else's baby. She actually *had* kidnapped the baby, but it turned out that the baby had been switched at birth and was Jazz's real son. Her lawyer had jumped up and shouted "Objection!" and then the medical records were brought in, proving everything, and Jazz got to go home with her little boy.

I swung my legs out of bed and headed into the bathroom to take a shower. I turned the water on as hot as I could make it without being burned. I put so much shampoo in my hair that the lather was really thick. It took a long time to wash it out. When I stepped out, the mirror was all fogged up, and my skin was pink from the hot water. I dried off, brushed my teeth, combed out my hair, and got dressed. To kill time I decided to blow-dry my hair instead of letting it air-dry. I went into Mom and Faux Pa's bathroom to get Mom's turbo hair dryer and round brushes, and then I brought them back to my room. I blew out my hair, trying my best to do it like at a hair salon, and then I put everything away. There was nothing left to do. I went back in my room and sat on my bed. It seemed dumb to watch TV or read a book, so I just stared off into space, like Faux Pa does sometimes. There was a beam of light coming in through the window, hitting the dust particles that were floating in the air, illuminating them. When I was little, Faux Pa told me how everything is made up of particles called molecules but they're so small you can't see them without a microscope. I thought dust particles were actually molecules. I was convinced I had some sort of bionic vision, since I could see them with my own eyes.

It's so funny the things you think up when you're a little kid.

Time passed slowly. I tried to take a nap, but I couldn't. It felt like the minutes were taking hours to pass. An hour felt like forever. Suddenly, there were voices downstairs. Someone shouted, "Carly!" It was Mom's voice. We'd been doing a lot of shouting from the bottom of the stairs lately. I ran down as quickly as my legs would take me and threw myself into her arms. I was so happy to see her! I'd never been so happy to see someone in my whole life!

I held on to Mom tightly. We were both crying a little bit. It felt like she'd been gone for much more than just one night. After we let go, Faux Pa introduced me to

Mom's lawyers—Dale Addie and Jamie Berkell. Dale was a woman and Jamie was a man. It seemed like it should be the other way around. Dale was noticeably older than Jamie. I wondered if she was his boss.

"I need to take a shower," Mom said.

Faux Pa nodded toward the lawyers. "They're here, Leigh," he said. "They're on the clock."

"I just spent the night in the dirtiest place I've ever been," Mom said. "Let me at least wash my face and brush my teeth."

Faux Pa nodded. I followed Mom upstairs. I kept staring at her, like she wasn't really real. She was dressed in the shirt she'd been wearing the day before, when the agents had come to the door. I watched her walk into the bathroom, brush her teeth and wash her face. She took off her old shirt and splashed water on her arms. She turned off the faucet and rolled on an extra amount of deodorant, and then she put on something new and clean. "Are you okay?" I asked.

"It's good to be cleaned up," she said, not really answering my question. I was sitting on her bed, and she sat down next to me. "I'm sorry about all this," she said. "You must have been so scared."

"It's not your fault," I said.

"I guess I should go downstairs," Mom said. "Dale and Jamie charge by the hour." I stood up to follow her, but she told me she didn't think I should sit with her and Faux Pa when they talked to the lawyers. "It's grown-up stuff," she said.

"Come on, Mom," I said. "I'm not a baby."

"Carly, please—it's been such an awful couple of days."

I felt bad for giving her a hard time. "Sorry," I said. "I'll stay up here."

"Thanks, honey," she said.

I settled down on Mom and Faux Pa's bed. The clock on the cable box read 1:12, which meant *Lovelock Falls* was on. Whenever I stayed home from school, I watched the show from one to two. I picked up the remote control and turned it on.

There was Ally playing Violet van Ryan. She was in a black dress, at the memorial service for Violet's best friend, Misty Briggs. Misty had fallen off a cliff. They had a funeral for her even though they never found the body. I was pretty sure that meant Misty would come back from the dead in a few months. Probably she'd have amnesia, and it would take a while for everyone to realize she was alive, and even longer for her to figure out who she was.

Violet's dress was kind of sexy for a memorial service. The episodes are filmed about six weeks in advance of them actually being on TV. When Mom picked it out, she wouldn't have had any idea about what was going to happen to her.

I watched Ally move across the screen. I wondered if she still needed me to babysit that weekend. It was only three days away. I hadn't talked to Mom about it since Vivette was arrested, but I didn't want to let Ally down if she was counting on me.

Mom's cell phone was on the bedside table. I pointed the remote toward the TV and pressed the mute button, and then I picked up the phone and scrolled through the contacts until I found what I was looking for: JARON, ALLY. That was the cool thing about Mom's cell phone—she had the numbers for almost everyone on *Lovelock Falls* stored in her address book. I dialed Ally's cell-phone number. In between filming Ally always talked on her phone. I figured there was a good chance she'd pick up, and if she didn't, I could leave a message. I just wanted her to know I hadn't forgotten about her. The phone rang once, twice. My palms started to sweat, and the phone felt slippery. I knew it was silly, but I started to wish I hadn't called her at all. I had to remind myself that we were still friends. That hadn't changed.

"Hello?" Ally said. My voice felt suddenly caught in my throat. "Hello?" she said again.

"Ally?" I said.

"Yes?"

"It's Carly," I said.

"Carly?" she said, like she still couldn't figure out who I was.

"Carly Wheeler," I told her.

"Oh, Carly," Ally said. "How are you?"

"I'm all right," I said. "My mom just got home."

"Good," she said. "That's really good. Listen, I'm in the makeup chair now, so I have to run. But honey, we probably shouldn't be talking right now—you know, for legal reasons. It's really complicated."

She paused for a second. *Complicated*, I thought. I wondered if Ally had asked her guru about it, and he had told her to simplify her life.

"Let's just wait until this resolves itself, okay?" Ally asked.

"Okay," I said.

"I'm thinking about you. I'm sure everything will work out just the way it's supposed to."

Ally was very into the way things were supposed to be. Her guru said everything happened for a reason. Sometimes I wasn't too sure about that. "I hope so," I said.

"Bye, honey," Ally said.

After I hung up, I realized I hadn't even asked Ally about Saturday. But if she didn't want to talk to me until everything was resolved, I knew that meant she didn't want to see me either. She had probably lined up another babysitter for Madison and Nicole, or maybe she was just going to take them to lunch with her. I was so mad at Vivette for messing everything up. I really wanted to go to Ally's house.

But the important thing, I reminded myself, was that Mom was home. She was downstairs with the lawyers, and they would figure everything out. Maybe it was possible it would be resolved, like Ally said, by the end of the day, and then I would get to go to Ally's on Saturday. I pressed the remote to turn the sound back on, but I didn't feel like watching *Lovelock Falls* anymore, so I changed the channel.

Mom came back upstairs a while later. She walked into the room, and her face looked blotchy. "Were you crying?" I asked.

She nodded. "Just a little," she said. "This is all very hard."

"I know," I said. "Are the lawyers still here?"

"They're leaving now," she said.

"Don't you think it's funny that the man is named Jamie and the woman is named Dale?" I asked. I wanted to make her laugh, the way she did when I was upset, but Mom just shrugged. She didn't seem like herself.

"I didn't really think about it," she said.

"What did they say about everything?" I asked. "Will you have to go back to court?"

"Yeah," Mom said.

"When?"

"I don't know yet, honey."

"But you won't have to go back to jail, right?"

Mom brought her hands to her face and rubbed her eyes. "Everything is a mess," she said.

Faux Pa had said the exact same thing that morning. It was a mess, but messes could be cleaned up. "The lawyers will resolve it," I said. "When do you think it will be resolved?"

"Honey, I don't know," Mom said.

"I called Ally about Saturday, but she wouldn't talk to me. She said we shouldn't talk until everything is resolved."

"You shouldn't call anyone from the show right now," Mom said.

"I don't understand any of this," I said. "It's about Vivette, right?"

"Yes, it's about Vivette," Mom said. She paused. "And they're accusing me of stealing from the show too."

"But that was Vivette! I heard you guys talking about it." I hoped Faux Pa wouldn't be mad at me for telling Mom. He'd told me to keep it to myself. But that couldn't mean I was supposed to keep it a secret from Mom, too. "You would never do that."

Mom's face twisted. "Oh, Carly," she said.

"No," I said. "You would never do that."

"I am so sorry," Mom said.

chapter eight

I know this is going to sound weird, but before Mom was arrested, I used to picture myself going through different kinds of emergencies. Maybe it was because I'd watched too many episodes of *Lovelock Falls*—the characters on the show are always in the middle of emergency situations. Or maybe I've just always had an active imagination. I would see myself in a horrible car accident, or a plane crash, or sick with a really bad disease. And then there I'd be, in a hospital bed, looking brave. All of my friends would call, and send cards, and visit. Other times I'd bring Mom and Faux Pa into it—they'd be the ones in a crash, and I would be an orphan. It's not like I wanted any of those things to happen. But in this really strange, twisted way, it was exciting to imagine the things that scared me the most. My heart would race, and I would feel like I was at the center of something.

Of course, I never told anyone that I thought about

these things. I'm sure if I had, they would have thought there was something wrong with me. I mean, who thinks an emergency is exciting? Besides, I really didn't think that anything bad would ever actually happen. But maybe I jinxed myself, because all of a sudden I was in the middle of a real emergency—one I couldn't have even imagined. My family was in the center of something, but I just wanted to go back to the way things were before.

I woke up late on Friday morning—my third straight day of not going to school. All week I had been home, not doing anything much. I had missed the history quiz and the next experiment in science, along with all my other classes. Instead, I watched TV and read a couple of chapters in *My Antonia*, the book we were reading for English. I stared into space, watching the dust particles, and listened to the phone ring.

The phone rang a lot. I didn't want to talk to anyone. My body felt strange. You know the feeling when you don't get enough sleep and you're so overtired that you can't even fall asleep—you just feel like you're walking through fog? That's how I felt. Faux Pa told me I shouldn't talk to any of my friends about what was going on, anyway.

Mostly, it wasn't my friends who called; it was the reporters. *Lovelock Falls* is such a popular soap opera, and it was big news that Mom had been arrested. For the first time ever, I wished Mom had a normal job at a regular, boring office. Of course, now she didn't have any job at all. She'd started spending a lot of time in her room with the door closed. Sometimes I walked up to the door and lifted my hand to knock, but there was something holding me back, like I was afraid of her, the way Justin was.

Faux Pa was really mad at Mom about everything, but I didn't know what I was feeling. I was just confused. It seemed like we were living in a fake life, like in a dream, even though there were newspaper articles that said it was all real. When I was a little kid, I thought it was possible that my dreams were actually my real life. I told Mom about my theory, and she said since life is consistent when we are awake, that is what is real. Dreams don't always make sense. But right then, being awake didn't seem to make sense: Those things Vivette had done weren't things my mother would do. Except she said she'd done them.

The newspaper was delivered to our house, the way it had been for as long as I could remember. Faux Pa had brought it inside and left it on the dining room table. He told me it would be better if I didn't read about it, but when he wasn't looking, I leafed through until I found what I was looking for. The headline: THE PLOT THICKENS—SECOND "LOVELOCK FALLS" STAFFER ARRESTED. Underneath, in smaller letters, was the name of the reporter who wrote it: Christine Barrett.

I read the article standing up. Mom's name was there, in print. It was so official. The article talked about how she lived in New Rochelle, was married, and had a daughter. It didn't name Faux Pa or me specifically, but there were lots of details about her job—what it meant to be a stylist on *Lovelock Falls*, how she'd been hired by Vivette Brooks and had worked there for eight years.

Now Wheeler and Brooks are accused of conspiring to embezzle funds from the show. On Tuesday, Wheeler's contract

with *Lovelock Falls* was terminated, and she was taken into custody by federal agents. The following day she pled not guilty to the charges and posted bail. The terms of her release include the surrender of her passport and restriction of travel to the tristate area.

When I finished reading, I folded the paper back up so it looked like I hadn't touched it at all. I wondered how Christine Barrett knew so much. When the reporters called, Faux Pa just said "no comment," and then hung up the phone.

I wandered into the den and sat down next to Faux Pa. "You know, Carly, you have to go to school on Monday."

"I don't know if I can." I couldn't imagine being able to concentrate in any of my classes. And I was embarrassed, too. Lots of people had the newspaper delivered to their houses: my friends, my teachers, and the kids I passed in the hall in between classes. Everyone would know what was going on. It was possible even the guys behind the counter at Slice of Life would know.

"If anyone asks you about Mom, just say you can't talk about it," he said.

"It's not that easy," I said. "I think it might be better if you just homeschooled me for a while." It wasn't even that crazy an idea—after all, he was a professor.

"You're right; it's not easy," Faux Pa agreed. "But I can't homeschool you—I'm only an expert in one subject, and you'd miss your friends. Besides, I have to go to work."

"Can we at least discuss it later?" I asked. Just so you

know, asking to discuss something later is generally a good strategy for getting your parents to give in. It makes you sound sort of mature and reasonable, and then it's possible that you'll eventually wear them down. But this time Faux Pa wasn't budging.

"I'm sorry, baby. But none of this is your fault. It has nothing to do with you."

The phone started ringing again. Faux Pa picked up the receiver and checked the caller ID before answering. The day before, he had called the phone company in order to block private callers from getting through. He didn't want to answer the phone and be surprised by a reporter on the other end. But I guess it was someone safe, because he pressed the button on the receiver and said, "Hi there."

It was Jocelyn calling. I could tell from Faux Pa's end of the conversation—he was saying something about Jessa and Justin, and how it was his year to have them for Thanksgiving and he still wanted them to be with us.

Thanksgiving—it was just a few weeks away. Obviously, Vivette and Ed wouldn't be with us this time around. Nothing would be the same. I didn't want to think about it anymore. I picked up the remote and turned the TV on, softly so as not to disturb Faux Pa. I flipped through the channels, not really trying to listen in on his conversation with Jocelyn, but still, I couldn't help but overhear. They were talking about Mom now. "God, Jocelyn," Faux Pa said. "I told you I can't talk about this." There was a pause; I guess Jocelyn was saying something back to him. Then he said, "I'm sorry. I just don't know what I'm going to do. I have absolutely no idea."

There was something soft and intimate about his

voice. It wasn't the way he usually spoke to Jocelyn. It made me uncomfortable. I couldn't just sit there and watch TV, so I stood up and went up to my room. It felt like there was something buzzing inside my head. I sat down on my bed and put my hands over my ears, but the noise wouldn't go away.

Faux Pa came up a few minutes later. He knocked on the door. I took my hands off my ears and told him to come in.

"Mom and I are headed over to the lawyers' office," he said. "We have a meeting at noon." His mouth was set straight; his lips looked thinner. I wondered what Jocelyn had been talking about when Faux Pa had said he had no idea. Maybe she'd asked Faux Pa if he was going to divorce Mom. What if he left for the lawyers' office and decided not to come back? I didn't think he would just abandon me like that, but then again, I didn't think my mom would ever embezzle money from *Lovelock Falls.*

If he left, I wouldn't be the only kid with divorced parents. *It happens every day,* I thought, which is the name of a Carly Simon song. But I'd be the only kid I know whose parents divorced for the reason mine did.

I just wanted everyone to be there with me, and to be the way they always were. I didn't want to be alone.

"This will probably take a couple hours," Faux Pa said.

"Can I go with you?" I asked.

He stood in the doorway, tall and lean. Sometimes he reminds me of a bird, the way his head seems to move ahead of his body, and the way his joints bend. He has the sharpest elbows I've ever seen. "I suppose so," he said.

We went downstairs. Mom was at the coat closet,

putting on her light-blue Burberry jacket. "We won't be too long," she told me.

"Faux Pa said I could go with you," I said. Mom looked past me and shot him a look.

"You dragged her into this," he said from behind me. "You changed all our lives. She heard you. You didn't know that, did you? She heard you and Vivette talking all about it."

"I know," Mom said. Her voice caught. I wondered if she was going to cry.

"You're dragging us all down with you," Faux Pa told her. He grabbed a jacket from the closet. "Come on; let's just go."

chapter nine

We didn't talk at all during the car ride over to the lawyers' office. I sat behind Mom, the way I always do when we're in the car all together. Faux Pa moves the seat way back, so there's barely any legroom behind his seat. Even though I'm tiny, I like to stretch out, and Mom is much smaller than Faux Pa. Everyone looked the same as they always did, but right there, sitting in the backseat, I realized I didn't even recognize my family.

We pulled up in front of a brick building with a sign that said AARONSON, BRESSLER & LOSQUADRO, ATTORNEYS AT LAW out front. "Well, we're here," Faux Pa said, breaking the silence.

"How come the sign doesn't say 'Addie and Berkell'?" I asked.

"Aaronson, Bressler, and Losquadro are the guys who founded the law firm," Faux Pa said. "I don't think they're even alive anymore. They just keep their names on the marquee."

We walked inside the building. Mom gave our names to the receptionist, who told us to take a seat. There were couches in the reception area. They looked soft, but when we sat down, it turned out that they weren't comfy at all.

Jamie Berkell came out a few minutes later. Mom and Faux Pa stood up, so I did too. Jamie shook all of our hands and led us into a conference room. Around the table were leather desk chairs, the kind with wheels on the bottom—when I was little, I used to love to sit in those chairs and spin around. I couldn't believe how much I was thinking about chairs.

The conference room door opened, and a woman stuck her head in. "Does anyone want something to drink—coffee, water, soda?"

My throat felt so dry, but Faux Pa and Mom shook their heads. "Debbie, why don't you bring a few waters in, just in case," Jamie said. The woman—Debbie—ducked back out to fetch the water. Jamie turned to us. "Dale will join us in a little bit," he said. "But she wanted us to get started first."

I looked up at him. He had dark hair that was slicked back, like it was oiled. It was funny that he had a girl's name, or not a girl's name exactly, but one that could go either way. There was something sort of gruff about Jamie. The way he moved wasn't smooth. I thought about other names for him—definite boys' names, like Ian or Mike or Andrew or Zach. He pulled a yellow notepad toward himself and jerked a pen across the top to make sure it was working.

"Leigh, let's go back through the time line," Jamie

said. "Tell me again: When did Vivette Brooks first approach you?"

Mom took a deep breath. "Hold on a moment," Faux Pa said. "Haven't we gone through all this already?"

"When we talked the first time, your wife was very emotional," Jamie said. "I need to make sure we didn't miss any details."

"I just don't see why we need to waste time and repeat things," Faux Pa said. "Not to mention the waste of money."

I always think it's funny when someone says "not to mention," because of course that means they are mentioning it.

"I know you're worried about our fees, but I assure you, this is important information to review. And remember, I'm an associate here, so my hourly rate isn't as high as a partner's, like Dale."

I remembered Mom and Faux Pa saying that the lawyers charged by the hour. I wondered how much it cost us to just be sitting there. Faux Pa was always more careful about money than Mom, and sometimes she would make fun of him about it. Like when he would talk about how expensive the meals at a restaurant were, she would smile and tell him his inner miser was coming out. The thing is, we weren't really rich, like Annie's family, but we had enough.

It was just one more thing that seemed to have suddenly changed about our lives. Mom wasn't saying anything about Faux Pa's inner miser. I wondered if we had to really be worried about money now. If we couldn't afford the attorneys, wouldn't one be appointed for Mom? That was what Special Agent Dixon Smith had said.

Debbie came back in and set four bottles of water on the table. I wondered if we would be charged if I drank one. We could still afford water, right? I was just so thirsty. I reached forward and grabbed a bottle, twisted the cap off, and took a sip.

"We won't have to go over this information again when Dale comes in?" Faux Pa asked.

"She may have some specific questions," Jamie said, "but I'll share my notes with her. Okay?"

"All right," Faux Pa said. He sat back in his chair.

Jamie nodded toward Mom. "Leigh," he said. "When did Vivette approach you?"

Mom looked over at me, and my stomach flip-flopped. She turned back toward Jamie. "It was a few months after I started working at *Lovelock Falls*," she said. "About seven and a half years ago."

"And you hadn't met Jonathan, your husband, at that time?"

"No," Mom said, "I hadn't."

"Tell me about your relationship with Vivette," Jamie said.

Mom shrugged, like she was a little kid and couldn't find the words.

"Leigh," Jamie said, "I know this is hard to talk about, but the more you can tell me, the better."

Mom sucked in her breath and let it out slowly. "Vivette's one of my closest friends," she said. "We just clicked. It happened very quickly—right after we met. You know how it happens when you meet someone, and you feel like you have so much in common. It's like you've known each other for a much longer period of time."

I knew what Mom meant—that's how it was with Annie and me. We shared a cookie on the first day of third grade, and that was it: We were best friends.

"Anyway," Mom said, "it was nice to have a friend like that. She was more like an older sister, actually. She was my confidante. You have to understand that working like that, so closely with people, it's like a big family. Vivette knew a lot about my personal life—that I was widowed, suddenly, when Carly was a baby. She knew I didn't have a lot of money, and I really felt like she was looking out for me—the way someone in your family would."

"And that's how it started?" Jamie asked.

"Yes," Mom said. "I was talking to Vivette one day—just the way we always did—and I mentioned how hard it was to keep up with expenses. Carly was getting older, and everything was adding up. I had had her enrolled at Preston Day School. It was what Randy—my first husband—and I had always planned to do. He had gone there himself. My mother was helping out, but then she became ill, and I had to put her in a nursing home. It was such a trying time. I had these neighbors, the Sarsens, who offered to loan me money. They tried to help me with my budget, but I just felt like I was drowning. I owed money to so many people. Vivette told me she sometimes made personal purchases on her corporate credit card. I had a corporate card too, and she told me to use it—just to pay for Carly's things, her clothing, stuff like that."

I looked down at what I was wearing—my good jeans and a long-sleeved black shirt with HEARTBREAKER written in red letters across the front. Mom had bought it for me in New York City. We had all gone into the city together that day—Mom, Faux Pa, Jessa, Justin, and me. Justin wanted to check out some video-game store, which Jessa and I had no interest in, so we split up into boys and girls. Faux Pa took Justin to his store, and Mom brought Jessa and me to Bloomingdale's. Jessa isn't really into shopping, but I guess she thought it was better than an hour in the game store. The saleswomen there all knew Mom. They hugged her hello, and told me how lucky I was to be her daughter, which made me feel proud. Mom said we could each get a few things. The only thing Jessa wanted was a hat that kind of looked like a train conductor's cap, but I got a bunch of things—the HEARTBREAKER shirt, a sweater dress, and a belt with patches on it. Then we met up with Faux Pa and Justin for lunch. It was a fun day. A totally normal, fun day. I wondered if we would ever have a day like that again. Right then, sitting in the lawyers' office listening to Mom, watching Jamie Berkell take notes on the things she said, it seemed impossible. It's not like the saleswomen would've hugged Mom hello if they'd known what she had done. They wouldn't have said I was lucky to be Mom's daughter.

My HEARTBREAKER shirt was one of my favorite shirts. I had worn it a lot so it had been washed a bunch of times and was really comfy, but right then my skin started to itch. I realized it might be stolen. I mean, it might have been bought with the money Mom stole from *Lovelock Falls*. In fact, every piece of clothing that I owned might not really belong to me.

"I—I—," Mom stuttered. "I'm not trying to make excuses. I knew it was wrong, but the way things were set up, no one besides Vivette would know. The show had such a big clothing allowance—especially in those days."

"So no one was watching the purchases you made on your corporate card? No one had to approve them?"

"Vivette had to approve them," Mom said. "She was the head of the department."

"Right," Jamie said.

It was the first time I was hearing the whole entire story. Jamie kept asking Mom questions. His voice was really calm and even, like he wasn't surprised or upset by anything she was saying. But she was my mother, and I didn't feel calm at all. I looked at Faux Pa. He was gripping the edge of the table.

Mom said she kept on using her corporate credit card to buy my clothes. At first she only bought what I needed, like if I grew out of my rain boots, she bought me another pair. And then, little by little, she started buying more stuff, clothing for herself, things we didn't really need. Vivette approved all the purchases. As time went by, Vivette and Mom figured out how to make more purchases on their corporate credit cards—not just clothing, but other things too.

"Can you give me some examples?" Jamie asked. "Furniture? Car payments?"

"Yes," Mom said. "Both of those things."

"How would you make a purchase from a store that wasn't a clothing store, like if you were making a car payment?" Jamie asked.

"Well, nobody was really looking over the records except for Vivette," Mom said. "And we were able to get cash advances from the cards."

"And Vivette approved the cash advances?" Jamie asked.

"Yes," Mom said. "She took cash advances too."

"I know we talked about this the other day, and you didn't have a number, but did you come up with an estimate—how much money you spent over the years on personal items for yourself and your family?"

"I think about a hundred and fifty thousand dollars," Mom said. "Maybe closer to two hundred thousand."

I gasped out loud. I couldn't help it. My hand knocked against my water bottle, and it spilled out onto the conference room table. We were probably being charged for the bottle, and now I had wasted Mom and Faux Pa's money. "Oh, no," I said. My voice came out like I was about to cry.

"That's all right, Carly," Faux Pa said.

"Of course it's all right," Jamie said. "We have napkins." He stood up and grabbed a bunch of napkins from the cabinet against the wall. "Here," he said, patting down the table. "Good as new."

"Thank you," I said.

"Do you want another bottle?" Jamie asked. I shook my head. This was going to be so expensive, and we had to save money. "All right, Leigh," he said, "We're going to emphasize that you were a widow, responsible for an elderly mother in a nursing home. And you were a single mother, raising a little girl."

"She's not a single mother anymore," Faux Pa said.

"No of course not," Jamie said. "You were married six years ago, is that correct?"

"Yes," Mom said.

"When did you meet?"

"The year before that," Mom said. "A mutual friend of ours had a housewarming party."

"And you never told Jonathan about what you and Vivette were doing?"

"No," Mom said. "I never told him. I never discussed it with anyone."

"Was money still an issue once you and Jonathan were married?" Jamie asked.

"Off and on," Mom said. "Jon was a professor at Pace when we got married, and you know, teachers never make enough. Then he left to join an engineering firm, which would've been more money, but the economy was bad, and there were layoffs. He was out of work for a few months. Eventually he landed back at Pace."

I felt dizzy. No one had ever told me that. Mom had told me he left the firm because he missed teaching. I wondered how many more lies there were in our family.

"Oh, sugar," Faux Pa said. His voice sounded angrier than I'd ever heard, but still he couldn't curse. "I'm sorry. So you're saying that this is my fault, Leigh?"

"No," Mom said. "I just wanted to preserve our lives—the quality of our lives. You had alimony and child-support payments to keep up with, and it was just so easy. I guess old habits die hard. I made a mistake."

I thought of Ally's guru: *There's no such thing as a mistake.*

"That's not an excuse, Leigh," Faux Pa said. "Just because it was easy and you wanted nice things—that's not enough. You could've lived with a smaller wardrobe, or driven an older car. Carly could have gone to public school." *But Preston is* my *school,* I thought. *How could he even talk about me going somewhere else?* "You didn't need to steal anything. We would've made do. We would've been just fine."

Mom started to cry. I watched her shoulders shaking, but I didn't move to comfort her. Jamie stood up to get another napkin from the cabinet. He put his hand on her shoulder. "This is hard," he said. He had this look of incredible understanding on his face. I wondered if that was something he learned in law school—how to look nice and compassionate so the criminals and their families would feel more comfortable. "We've covered enough for now," Jamie said. "I'll give you all a few minutes and let Dale know we're ready for her."

Jamie left the room, and the three of us just sat there. I had a feeling Faux Pa would have said more if I wasn't there. Mom wiped her face and blew her nose, making an ugly honking sound. In school I never blow my nose in front of people, because it always sort of embarrasses me, but Mom just did it like she didn't care. She wasn't my cool, pretty mother anymore. I had always thought my mom was such a good person. I thought she was better than other people's moms, but I'd been wrong about her that whole time. She'd been stealing money for years. I bet no one else I knew had a mother who had ever done that. It was so much money. I felt like I didn't know her at all.

Mom stood up to throw the napkin away, and then walked to the window. It's not like there was a good view of anything. It just looked out onto the back of the parking lot. She pressed a palm against the glass. I wondered if she felt locked in, like in a jail cell.

A few minutes later there was a knock on the door, and then Jamie came back in with Dale. Mom sat down again. She, Faux Pa, and I were on one side of the table. Jamie and Dale were on the other side, as if we were on opposing teams. They started talking about legal strategies. "We have a number of different options, but I can't offer you any guarantees, Leigh," Dale said. "I can't promise you an outcome. All I can do is advise you of the risks and benefits of each choice, so you can make an informed decision."

"Okay," Mom said.

"First of all, we could go to trial. Remember, the burden of proof is on them."

"Meaning?" Mom asked.

"Meaning you're innocent until proven guilty. You have a right to a jury trial, and we may get lucky with a sympathetic jury. There is some chance that the prosecutor wouldn't be able to prove your guilt and you would be acquitted, or even that the case would be dropped. That's the best-case scenario."

Sitting there at the conference table, I realized my American Government & Law class was going to come in handy. Because of Mrs. Harrity, I knew exactly what Dale Addie was talking about. The jury would be a random group of people who sat in the courtroom and listened to the whole case. They would decide whether Mom was innocent or guilty. If Mom was acquitted, it meant the jury had decided she was innocent. But the prosecutor was the person trying the case against Mom, and he was going to try to convince the jury that Mom was guilty.

"Do you think there's a good chance of us actually realizing the best-case scenario?" Faux Pa asked.

"Frankly, no," Dale said.

"So what's the worst-case scenario?"

"The worst is that we lose at trial, the jury takes a hard look at what you did and recommends a harsh sentence to the judge. The judge could decide to throw the book at you—because this involves a TV show, it's somewhat of a high profile case, and he may want to make an example of you. He could give you a stiff sentence—the maximum for the crime."

"Jail," Mom said.

"No, prison, actually," Dale said. "Jail is just a

short-term facility, for people awaiting trial. Prison is a long-term facility, for inmates who have been convicted of crimes."

"Otherwise known as the pen, or the clink, or the slammer," Mom said. She cracked a smile, like suddenly she was back to being her old self—someone who made jokes to lighten the mood. I wanted to tell her it wasn't funny, that it didn't matter what she called it. It was still a place she might be locked away. I pictured Mom behind bars. I wondered if I would get to visit her in prison. Would she be behind one of those glass windows, where we could see each other but not touch? I'd seen it on TV—you had to pick up a phone to talk to the person on the other side, because the glass was too thick to hear through.

"Yes," Dale said. "But the second option is for me to call the prosecutor and arrange for you to take a guilty plea. We can avoid a jury trial entirely. You stand up and admit guilt, and accept responsibility for your actions, and the prosecutor will likely recommend a more lenient sentence. Of course, I can't promise that the judge will actually impose a lighter sentence. But there are a number of factors that the judge may look favorably on—this is your first offense, and you don't have a prior record."

"Is that what you would do?" Mom asked, back to being serious again.

"It's not important what I would do," Dale said. "You have to figure out what you're most comfortable with—what you can live with."

I wondered how Mom was living with any of it.

"Excuse me, Dale," Faux Pa said, "I know you're being careful not to tell us what to do, but what do you *think*?

You must have seen cases like this before. What kind of time is Leigh facing?"

"Most likely, it's twelve to eighteen months."

"Twelve to eighteen months in prison?" I asked. I didn't mean to call out like that, and I was sort of surprised to hear myself speak. They all looked at me. I knew my face was turning red, because I could feel my cheeks burning. "That's so long—that's more than a school year!" I hadn't expected it to be so much time. Even though Mom had taken a lot of money, the idea of living without her for so long seemed crazy.

"Carly, honey, please don't make this any harder," Mom said. "Do you want to wait for us in the reception area?"

I shook my head. "No," I said. "I want to stay."

Faux Pa reached over and put his hand on my hand. He rubbed his thumb against my thumb.

"It's the range we get, looking at the sentencing guidelines, based on the crime and the amount of money involved," Dale explained. "It can go above or below that. Hopefully, with a guilty plea, the judge will sentence you in the lower end. He may look favorably on your acceptance of responsibility and go even further below the guidelines. Certainly we can hope for probation, or time in a halfway house. I don't know what's going to happen. I just want you to be prepared that you are, most likely, facing some time in prison. This is a white-collar crime, not a violent crime, so we will recommend a minimum-security facility—that all goes in the sentencing memo."

I didn't know what a sentencing memo was, but Mrs. Harrity had taught us about white-collar crime. Basically, in a white-collar crime there weren't any weapons and no one died, but money was still involved.

"I see," Mom said.

"Listen, it's not my style to sugarcoat anything," Dale said. "I want you to make informed decisions. Once you make the decision to plead guilty, there's no turning back. There's no chance of acquittal. But the prosecution does have evidence against you, so there's a good chance we'd lose at trial—and we could lose big. The other drawback, of course, is the expense—a trial takes longer, and our fees go up accordingly."

"How expensive will it be?" Faux Pa asked.

"I can't give you an exact number," Dale said. "Trial prep is very arduous—there are documents to review, exhibits, and witnesses to prep, and we'll have to prepare to cross-examine their witnesses."

"Who do you think they'll call as witnesses?" Mom asked.

"Anyone who may have information about the case," Dale said. "People who had reason to believe you and Vivette were engaging in criminal activity."

"What about my family?" Mom asked.

"There's a spousal privilege," Dale said. "Even if Jonathan had reason to believe you were embezzling funds, he does not have to testify against you."

"And Carly?"

"There is no parent-child privilege," Dale said. "Does Carly have information about the case?"

My heart started to pound. *This has gone on too long. Jonathan has no idea.* "She and her friend Annie heard Vivette and me talking once," Mom said. "Could this get ugly? I don't want the girls to be involved."

"This is already ugly," Faux Pa said.

I pictured Cruella questioning Annie and me, in a

courtroom just like the one on *Lovelock Falls. Objection!* Dale would shout. "We'll try to keep them out of it," Dale said. "There's no reason to think the prosecution would even suspect Carly or her friend knew anything."

"But if Leigh pleads guilty, then no one would have to testify," Faux Pa said.

"That's right," Dale said.

Faux Pa shook his head. "Sugar," he said again. "I never liked Vivette Brooks."

"Oh, Jonathan," Mom said.

"I'm serious, Leigh," he said. "She was your friend, and I never would have said anything. But I always knew she had something up her sleeve."

"I wish it didn't have to be this way," Mom said.

"What's going to happen to her?" I asked.

"Do you mean Vivette?" Dale asked.

"Yeah," I said.

"I spoke to her lawyer this morning," Dale said. "She's weighing her options too. It looks like she's in much deeper than your mother. There's more money involved where she's concerned."

"You're not her lawyer?" I asked.

"No," Dale said. "It would be a conflict of interest for me to represent both your mom and Vivette."

"Why?" I asked.

"Because they're accused of conspiracy—of conspiring together to commit a crime."

"You mean embezzlement," I said.

"Right," Dale said. "When you use money that's not your own."

"I know what it is," I said.

"Okay," Dale said. She seemed to look at me a little more seriously, like I wasn't just a little kid. "Well, in the event we do go to trial, your mother may know things about Vivette that could help our case—things that could be used against Vivette. If I were representing Vivette as well, I wouldn't want to bring that to the judge's attention. But you don't need to worry about her. She has a very good lawyer representing her."

"I wasn't worried," I said.

"All right," Dale said. She turned back to Mom. "Leigh, aside from your husband and your daughter, have you discussed this with anyone?"

Mom shook her head. "The phone has been ringing off the hook," she said. "Mostly reporters. I guess this is the time when you learn who your true friends are."

"That's funny, Leigh," Faux Pa said. "You haven't exactly been 'true' to anyone."

"I think we can wrap this up for the day," Dale said. "You should go home and discuss everything together, as a family. I know the decision to go to trial or plead guilty is intensely personal. Let's be in touch over the next couple of days."

We stood up, shook hands, and said good-bye. I followed Mom and Faux Pa down the hall to the front door. Past the woman named Debbie who'd given us the bottled water, and the receptionist who'd called to tell Jamie when we arrived. I knew everyone in the office must know who we were: the criminal, her husband, and their daughter. It was like we were somehow marked. I wished I could be invisible. I wished I really did have a Visibility Zapper pill to swallow so I could just disappear.

chapter ten

I went back to school the next week. Mom and Faux Pa told me not to say anything about what was going on, but of course everyone knew. I wondered if it would be better to be unpopular, like Ginny Winkler. Nobody ever really notices her. I was used to people looking at me, but in a different kind of way—in a way like they sort of wanted to be me. I was cool; I was Annie Rothschild's best friend. Now I was probably the only student at Preston to ever see her mother get arrested. When I walked down the hall, I knew everyone was thinking about it.

People weren't mean to me, at least not out loud. They would ask, "How are you?" as if they were really concerned. I knew they just wanted to know the gossip. I pretended everything was fine. I said that the lawyers were working it out, like it was all a big misunderstanding.

I felt so strange, almost like I was two different

people. On the outside I kept acting like my regular, normal self. But on the inside I was so scared, and I couldn't stop thinking about it. And the worst part was what was going on between Annie and me. I couldn't explain it. I mean, we were still friends. We had lunch together every day—Annie, Lauren, Jordan, and me, just like always. But things *felt* different.

It was the little things, like she hadn't offered me her class notes from the days I was absent. In sixth grade I missed a week and a half of school because I had appendicitis. Annie made a big deal about collecting all my assignments for me—even from the classes we didn't have together. On the day I went back to school, she put a WELCOME BACK, CARLY sign up on my locker. It wasn't that I expected the same kind of thing when I got back to school after Mom was arrested, but Annie didn't even offer to share her notes from math and history, the classes we had together.

I thought about what Annie had said about Vivette: *She was arrested. She had to have been doing something wrong. People don't just get arrested out of the blue.* She must've just known that Mom was guilty. I just wished she hadn't been there to see everything—when Mom and Vivette were talking, and when the FBI came to the door—because that made it so much worse. I was sure she'd told other people about it.

On Thursday, my fourth day back at school, I came out of the bathroom, and Annie and Jordan were standing in the hallway with these two other girls, Molly Anders and Jill Galin—eighth graders. Annie and Jordan weren't even really friends with them, but the thing about our school is that it's on the small side, so everyone knows everyone else. Everyone knows everyone else's parents, too—especially my mom, because of the whole thing with Carrie and Michelle and the Parents' Council. Now they were going to know my mom because she was a criminal.

The door to the bathroom is really heavy, and the hinge squeaks when you open it, so the four of them turned and saw me. Parents pay a lot of money to have their kids go to Preston Day School. You'd think the school administration would spring for some oil so the hinges wouldn't squeak.

I walked past them toward my locker, and they were all just silent. My cheeks felt hot. I wanted to cry right there. It was so obvious that they had just been talking about Mom, and that they were waiting until I was gone before they got back into their conversation. *Come on*, I thought. *It's been over a week. Haven't you guys talked about this enough already?* I wished something scandalous would happen to someone else, so my life wouldn't be the most interesting thing to gossip about.

Somehow I felt like I'd done something wrong too, just because I was Mom's daughter. Standing there, looking at Annie and the girls, I had a terrible thought: Maybe I would become unpopular, like Ginny Winkler. Maybe I had jinxed myself when I had secretly wished for it. I just had to make sure that I didn't start doing anything outwardly strange, like talking to myself in that way Ginny did, or something like that. That would seal my unpopularity for sure.

"Hey, Carly," Jordan said, like things were totally normal.

"Hey," I said. Part of me wanted to get away as fast as I could so they could just get on with talking about my family, but the other part of me wanted to stick around until the bell rang, so they wouldn't be able to. It seemed so rude. But I knew that if it had been someone else's mother, I probably would've gossiped about it too, because that's what we did. Not to be mean, but because those things are kind of interesting.

Except I didn't think I would do that to Annie. Actually, I was sure that I wouldn't. I'd never told anyone about the times I'd seen her mother drunk, because she was my best friend.

"Can I talk to you a sec?" I asked her.

Jordan, Molly, and Jill looked down, like they were embarrassed. But Annie looked straight at me, which was just so Annie. She never seems to be afraid or ashamed and that makes her kind of scary. "Sure," she said.

She followed me down the hall. I turned the dial on my locker and opened it so I could trade my English book for my science one. "Listen," I said, lowering my voice. "I know you guys are talking about my mom. Can you please just stop?"

"We weren't talking about her," Annie said. "Don't be paranoid."

"I'm not," I said.

"You are," Annie insisted.

I knew it was possible I had just been making things up in my head, the way I did sometimes. But then I thought about how different things were. "You haven't even really called me since it happened," I told her.

"What are you talking about?"

"You know," I said. "We used to talk every night."

"I talked to you last night," Annie said.

"Yeah, but I called you; you didn't call me," I said.

"So?" she asked. "I've called you lots of other times.

I don't exactly keep track of who calls who." She made me feel sort of dumb, but that's what it's like to argue with Annie. It's better to be on her good side.

"We only spoke for a couple seconds," I reminded her. "Then you said you had to go. You didn't even call me back."

"My mom needed me for something," Annie said. "Besides, I was going to see you in school anyway."

"I guess," I said.

"See," she said. "It's not a big deal."

"It's a big deal to me," I said.

"Come on, Carly," Annie said. "Don't be like that. The stuff with your mom will be fine. That's what I told my mom."

"What do you mean?"

"Don't worry about it," she said. "I'll call you tonight. Just relax, okay?"

"Fine," I said.

I closed my locker and walked into the science lab just before the bell rang. I took my seat, but then I realized I'd forgotten to take my science book out of my locker. How dumb was that? I didn't want to turn around and go back for it. Annie and the other girls might still be there in the hall. I hoped I didn't get in trouble. Our teacher, Dr. Sherman, was strict about things like that. He's sort of old-fashioned, although he's not evil like Mrs. Harrity. I actually think he likes what he does and wants us to be excited about learning. It's just that he's the oldest teacher at Preston, and he's got ideas about how things should be.

Dr. Sherman looks his age too. There are deep creases in his forehead, and his eyes are kind of buried under folds of skin. Sometimes, when I look at really old people, I wonder what they looked like when they were young, before they had wrinkles and those strange purplish spots they get from too much time in the sun.

My grandmother has those spots up and down her arms. Mom calls them "age spots." For some reason they make me think of the rings in a trunk of a tree, and the way you can tell how old a tree is by how many rings there are.

When Mom moved Grandma into the nursing home, she put up all these pictures. There on the windowsill are framed photos in chronological order from left to right: Grandma as a toddler, with her long, dark curls; in her white uniform the day she graduated from nursing school; next to Grandpa on their wedding day; then Grandma, Grandpa, and Mom, when Mom was a little girl; and finally, Grandma holding me on the day I was born. I don't have any memories of my grandmother being like the person in the picture—someone who held me up like she was showing me off. You can tell she knew who she was, and who I was. But by the time I was in first grade, she'd started forgetting things. Now she didn't even remember who I was.

Mom said she wanted the aides in the nursing home to see Grandma's individuality, to treat her like a person and not just another patient. That's why she put up the pictures. Sitting there in the science lab, remembering that, made my heart beat a little faster. It seemed like a long time since I'd thought anything nice about Mom. Anyway, the point was that Grandma looked completely different as an old person than she had when she was young, and I'm sure Dr. Sherman did, too.

Alex breezed into class and sat down next to me. We don't have desks in the science lab; instead there are tables made of this special black material. Dr. Sherman says it makes them nonflammable, but I'm still nervous whenever we have to use the Bunsen burners.

"Hey, Carly," Alex said. "What's shaking?"

"Absolutely nothing," I said.

"I don't believe that," he said. He grinned at me in that way of his. I was sure he was thinking about Mom. That's all anyone thought about these days when they saw me.

"Settle down, ladies and gentlemen," Dr. Sherman said. He always calls us "ladies and gentlemen," as if we're the audience at a circus. I turned toward him and made myself pay attention. "I have a feeling that today's lab is going to be everyone's favorite," Dr. Sherman continued. "Please turn to page ninety-six in your texts and work with your partners on this. The supplies you'll need are in the back cabinet, and the lab reports will be due on Monday."

"I forgot my book," I told Alex quietly.

"No worries," he said. "We can share." He flipped open his textbook and slid it over a little so I could see too. "Oh, sweet," he said. "The popcorn experiment."

I looked at the heading on the top of the page: "The How and Why of Popcorn's Pop." The instructions said we would need to use a Bunsen burner. Obviously—we'd have to heat up the kernels to make them pop. I shook my head. "What?" Alex asked.

"Nothing," I said. "I'll go get the supplies."

I had to make two trips to get everything we needed—the popcorn kernels, a beaker, a mount, and a Bunsen burner. Dr. Sherman reminded everyone to remain calm and orderly. Alex set everything up on the table; then he flicked the switch to turn on the Bunsen burner. The gas that comes out of that thing before you light it smells so awful—it smells like danger to me. I guess it's embarrassing to be such a wimp about it, especially since Faux Pa works in a college science department. He's around Bunsen burners all the time, and nothing's ever happened to him. But I can just imagine there being some story on the news—EXPLOSION IN SEVENTH-GRADE SCIENCE LAB DUE TO BUNSEN BURNER GAS LEAK. Alex lit a match and held it up to the gas, and all of a sudden there was a flame.

"I think it's cool how fire can change colors," Alex said. "I heard the hotter it is, the bluer the flame."

"Turn the gas down a little," I said. "The book says that if the fire is too hot, it might crack the beaker."

"It'll be okay," Alex said. "Relax."

I thought of Annie when he said that. In my head I heard her voice telling me the same thing: *Just relax, okay?* How could it be possible for me to relax with everything that was going on?

"So, Carly," Alex said. "I have a question for you."

Alex was one of the only people who hadn't yet asked me about my mom. But I had a feeling that was about to change.

"What?" I said.

"You know your friend Lauren?" he asked. I nodded. I wondered what Lauren had to do with Mom. Maybe Alex had the story mixed up, and he thought Lauren was the one who was there when the FBI came to our door. Annie would probably be upset if she knew that. She would want Alex to know that she saw it all happen, like it made her cool or important or something. Then I felt guilty for thinking that sort of thing about my best friend.

"So," Alex said, "what does she think of me?"

"You mean Annie, right?"

"No," Alex said. He looked at me funny. "Lauren."

"Oh," I said, surprised. I just assumed Annie was the one he would like most out of my friends, even though Lauren *is* very pretty and smart. She's taking Algebra I with the eighth graders this year, while the rest of us seventh graders are in Pre-Algebra. She's also in the eighth-grade French class. But she's not stuck-up at all about it, and everyone likes her and respects her. Sometimes I wonder what it's like to be Lauren, because she's different from the rest of us. It's cool to be smart at our school, but Lauren is beyond smart. Also, she's the only Korean kid in our grade. The thing about Lauren is that she doesn't seem to be afraid of what other people think.

"I don't really know what Lauren thinks of you," I told Alex. "She's never said."

"I thought girls talked about everything with their friends."

I wondered, *If you're the best-looking guy in school, do you just assume that all the girls talk about you?* I mean, the truth was that we did all talk about him. But it seemed sort of obnoxious for him to just think that.

"We have a lot of things to discuss besides you," I said. I was impressed with myself for coming up with a good answer so quickly.

"Is that so?" Alex asked.

"Uh-huh," I said. The popcorn started popping. I knew from page 96 of Alex's textbook that it was a chemical reaction. But still, it looked like magic. These little kernels at the bottom of the beaker all of a sudden exploding into white puffs.

"I'm glad we're friends," Alex said. "You're a cool girl, Carly Wheeler."

It was the first time since Mom was arrested that I actually thought maybe I was cool. It made me smile. "Thanks," I said. "You're cool too."

Alex grinned his grin. "I can't wait until we can eat," he said. "I'm starving."

I waited to see if he would say something else about Lauren—like ask me to ask her about him—but he didn't. I guess that was a good thing, because it would've been really complicated. Annie had been the first to say she was into Alex, so it was like she'd claimed him. But can you really claim a person? In a way I sort of felt sorry for Annie. She would be so sad if she knew. She'd be angry about it too. I realized there was a part of me that was glad about that, because she'd hurt my feelings.

"Oh, we're such excellent chefs," Alex said. "This popcorn is totally ready to eat."

He turned off the Bunsen burner, but we had to wait for the beaker to cool down before we could reach in.

chapter eleven

Mom and I have always had this bedtime tradition. I know it sounds babyish, but she always comes into my room to tuck me in. It started when I was little. She would sit on the edge of my bed, and we'd talk for a few minutes, and then she'd hug me good night. Afterward, I would lie down, and she'd pull the comforter over me and smooth it out. Now having her tuck me in felt weird and fake. She still came in to say good night, but I wasn't really into talking to her anymore. When she left, I had a hard time falling asleep. I knew Faux Pa was sprawled out on the couch in the den. He didn't want to sleep in the same room as Mom anymore.

One night I was thirsty, and I went downstairs after Mom had already come in to say good night. You can see into the den from the front hall. I saw Faux Pa's pillow and blanket on the ottoman, but he wasn't in there. Where was he? Carly Simon's voice floated into my head: *It happens every day*. I walked back toward the kitchen, and there he was, at the dining room table. He was just sitting there, rolling a pencil back and forth, back and forth, along the tabletop.

"Hi," I said.

"Oh, Carly," he said, "what are you doing up?"

"Nothing," I said. "I was thirsty. Are you working?"

"I'm just thinking," he said. He patted the table next to him. "Why don't you sit down? I'll get you some water."

I pulled out a chair and sat down. He brought me water in a coffee mug—one Mom had bought Jessa as a joke. It said, I KNOW WHAT MY PROBLEM IS—WHAT'S YOURS? I don't know if Jessa thought it was funny. I took a sip of water and put the mug down on the table. "What do you think she should do?" I asked.

"What do you mean?" Faux Pa asked.

"Do you think Mom should plead guilty?" She had to decide soon—at least that's what Dale and Jamie said.

"I don't know," he said. "It's impossible to know the right thing to do."

"My whole life you guys said telling the truth was the right thing," I reminded him. "Don't you think it's a little weird that Mom can't decide whether or not to tell the truth herself?"

"I know this is confusing," Faux Pa said. "We've always expected honesty from you, and here your mother has been lying all these years. It's very hypocritical."

"Don't worry," I said. "I'm not going to ever do what she did."

"I know you won't," he said. "I'm absolutely certain of it."

"If she goes to trial, and the judge asks her if she

stole from the show, will she just lie? Isn't that even more illegal?"

"When you are sworn in as a witness in court, you take an oath to tell the truth," Faux Pa said. "If you lie, you can be held in contempt of court, and that carries its own penalties. But if your mother went to trial, she probably wouldn't take the stand. She doesn't have to, you know."

"Yeah," I said. "I learned about this in my American Government class. It's part of the right to remain silent, I think." Faux Pa nodded. "But the part I don't get is," I continued, "if she doesn't take the stand, doesn't that look bad? Doesn't that look like she has something to hide?"

"Supposedly, the judge and jury aren't allowed to take that into account when they decide if she's innocent or guilty."

"Everyone already thinks she's guilty," I said. "You know the way they write about her in the paper. People think that at school, too."

"How are things at school?" Faux Pa asked. "How are your friends handling this?"

I shrugged. I felt awkward. It's not like Faux Pa and I don't talk about things, because we did. But I didn't think he would understand what it meant to be popular, and anyway, I was used to talking about my friends with Mom. I was afraid that when everyone found out that Mom had really taken the money, I wouldn't have any friends left at all. Sometimes I wondered if Annie was just friends with me because she got to come to the *Lovelock Falls* set and meet Ally Jaron. It was a horrible thing to think about my best friend. But still. "I just wish I could tell everyone it wasn't true and really mean it," I said.

"I feel exactly the same way," Faux Pa said.

"Do you still love her?" I asked.

"Oh, Carly."

I never would have thought it was possible for Faux Pa to stop loving Mom. We had had the perfect family. Why did she have to mess it all up?

"I won't be mad if you say you don't," I told him. "It's awful what she did. But does it count that she told Vivette she wanted to stop? Remember, I heard her say it had gone on too long."

"I have a lot of feelings about your mother right now," Faux Pa said. "I'm sorting them all out. I'm sure you are too."

"Yeah," I said.

"You should get up to bed," he said. He stood up and put a hand on my shoulder. He didn't answer my question.

chapter twelve

Jessa and Justin came over that weekend. Of course Faux Pa had told them about Mom's arrest and the charges against her, but he hadn't told them Mom was actually guilty.

Justin had a lot of questions, which he only asked if Mom wasn't in the room, like why the FBI would think that Mom had done it, and whether or not they were looking for the person who really did. Jessa didn't say much about it at all, except when she first walked in, she took me aside and said, "I'm sorry. I've been reading about it in the paper. This must really suck for you."

I nodded. "Thanks," I said.

"My mom feels bad for you too," she said. "She wanted me to tell you she's thinking of you."

Jessa and I didn't really ever talk about her mom. It was kind of a strange thing. Jessa was my stepsister, and my mother was her stepmother, but there wasn't any word to describe how Jocelyn and I were related. I guess we weren't related at all. I always figured that Jocelyn didn't like Mom or me; after all, Faux Pa had divorced her, and now he was living with us. Somehow that made Mom seem better than Jocelyn. But now my mother was the one accused of breaking the law. I doubted anything like that had ever happened to Jessa's mom.

I looked at Jessa. She was wearing a long gray sweater and black leggings. Generally, she always has something black on. She isn't one of those goth girls—you know, the ones with black clothes and the weird eye makeup. But there's something really intense about her all the same. I didn't know what to say back to her. "Tell your mom I said hi," I said. As soon as the words were out of my mouth, I realized I sounded totally lame.

Jessa nodded solemnly. "I will," she said.

On Saturday Justin had a hockey game, and Faux Pa went to watch him play. He dropped Jessa off at the library, one of her favorite places. That day she was meeting her friend Reese there. I'd met Reese a couple of times, and I could tell why she and Jessa were friends. First of all, they look alike. I know that sounds like a dumb reason to be friends with someone, but I do think it sometimes works that way, like how all the good-looking boys in school are friends with each other. And, more importantly, Jessa and Reese have similar personalities. Whenever I'm around the two of them, they don't seem to talk to each other that much, but I think that's just the way they like to be. Once, Reese spent the night at our house. She and Jessa camped out downstairs. I went to the kitchen to get a glass of water, and I peeked into the den. They were awake, but instead of talking or watching TV like Annie and I usually do at our sleepovers, they were sitting on opposite ends of the couch, reading.

With Faux Pa, Jessa, and Justin gone, it was just Mom and me in the house. She was in her room, and I was downstairs. I had called Annie and left a message on her cell phone. Then I called her at home, and her mom picked up. She said Annie couldn't come to the phone because she was studying for a history quiz. We're in the same class, so I knew she didn't really have a history quiz. I wondered if Annie was avoiding me. Sometimes when Mrs. Rothschild drinks too much wine, she gets confused about things.

"Can you just tell her I called?" I asked.

"Of course, darling," Mrs. Rothschild said. "She may not get back to you right away, though. I know she has a lot of work to do."

It was hard to tell by her voice if she was drunk. "Thanks," I said.

I felt lonely, but I didn't want to go upstairs and talk to Mom. When we talked about the case, I got upset and angry. And when we tried to talk about normal things, I felt the same way.

I decided to walk across the street to Amelia's. I left Mom a note on the dining room table—*Going out for a little while. I'll be back later. Carly*—and went to the hall closet to get my jacket. That morning Faux Pa had told Justin to bundle up, so I knew it would be cold out. Somehow that made things seem worse.

I pulled my purple pea coat and gray scarf out of the closet. Violet van Ryan had worn the scarf on last year's New Year's episode, when she had stood by the giant waterfall with Kyle Shepherd—he was about to propose to her for the second time, and he said this line that was really cheesy: "It would be impossible to measure the water in Lovelock Falls, and it would be impossible for me to measure all the ways I love you." Violet pressed up against him, and they kissed. The coat Violet was wearing had a fur collar. Mom told me that they'd gotten complaints from animal rights activists when the episode aired, and Ally said she didn't want Violet to wear fur anymore. At the time I thought about how strange it was that Mom's job was so public—she put a coat on Ally, and then she got hate mail from total strangers. It made me uncomfortable, but looking back it seemed like such a little thing. Now people hated Mom for something so much worse.

I buttoned up my coat and started winding the scarf around my neck. I used to love when Mom got me clothing from *Lovelock Falls*. I wondered if my scarf counted as stolen, if Mom had bought it for the show. It wasn't like she'd purchased it just for me, but just in case, I decided to leave it at home.

Amelia's house is diagonally across the street from ours. The first time I ever crossed a street by myself was to visit Amelia. I was almost eight, and Mom had stood at our front door and watched me, making sure I looked both ways and got safely to the other side and into Amelia's house. Now I felt weird because I hadn't called first. Amelia didn't always call ahead when she came to my house, but I realized the last time she'd come over was before Mom was arrested, so it was possible that things were different now.

I rang the bell anyway. It makes the same *ring RING ring* sound that our doorbell does, just in a slightly higher tone. Amelia swung the door open a few seconds later. Her hair was wet, so it looked darker than usual. When it's dry, she has kind of dirty-blond hair, but now it looked totally brown. "Hey!" she said.

"Hi," I said. "Is it okay that I came over?"

"Of course," she said. "Come on in." She took my hand and pulled me inside. "Did you eat lunch yet? I'm starving—are you starving?"

Amelia is always either famished or stuffed, never anything in between. She has this thing called celiac disease. It's not catching or anything like that, but it means she's allergic to gluten—an ingredient that's in just about everything. She has to be on a special diet, and it's really a drag. Sometimes I feel guilty eating in front of her, because she can't eat regular things, like pasta or sandwiches.

"I'm sort of hungry," I said. I followed her into the kitchen. It has an extra freezer for all of Amelia's special food—gluten-free pizza and waffles. I've had some of her food before, and it always tastes kind of strange—like it almost tastes normal, but a little more dense, so you know it isn't quite what it should be. I took off my coat and draped it across the back of one of the dining room chairs.

"Do you want a sandwich?" Amelia asked. "Billy and my mom actually baked a loaf of bread the other day, if you want to try it. They swear it tastes better than what you can buy in a store. Of course, I wouldn't know, because I can't eat any of it." Billy is Amelia's younger brother. I always feel weird eating bread in front of Amelia, since she isn't allowed to eat it herself—bread has gluten in it. I know Mr. and Mrs. Sarsen and Billy have gluten bread in front of Amelia the time, but it just seems rude.

"What are you having?" I asked.

"Salami and cheese," she said. She pulled the cold cuts out of the fridge along with a bottle of mustard and squirted some mustard out on a plate. Then she rolled up a piece of meat with a piece of provolone and dipped it into the mustard. I knew it would taste better on a sandwich, but I decided to eat it her way.

Amelia moved the plate of mustard over so it was directly in between us. "Thanks," I said.

"If you want, we can make cookies after this. My mom found a new recipe that I can actually eat, and supposedly it tastes really good." Amelia and I had stopped our quest for the perfect cookie when her celiac disease was diagnosed. It was just too hard, but her mom was always looking for new gluten-free recipes. Sometimes she would cook in the middle of the day, just to test out new recipes. Then we'd all taste whatever she'd made to see whether it was actually edible.

"Where is everyone now, anyway?" I asked.

"My dad actually had to work today, so he's in the city," Amelia said. "And my mom took Billy over to his friend Griffin's house. What's your family up to?"

"Jessa and Justin are here this weekend, so my stepfather is at Justin's hockey game, and Jessa's at the library. My mom is home. I don't really know what she's doing today."

"So," Amelia said, her voice softer, like she was trying to be careful, "how is your mom?"

"She's okay," I said.

"My mom didn't want me to bother you guys," Amelia said. "That's why I didn't come by for the last few days."

I wondered if that was part of the problem with Annie, too—maybe she didn't call me back because she was afraid she'd be intruding. I knew it was wishful thinking, but I hoped that was all it was.

"That's all right," I told Amelia.

"My mom and I have been talking about you guys," she said.

"A lot of people are talking about us," I said.

"I didn't mean in a bad way," Amelia said. "I just feel so bad for you guys. For your mom, especially. If that happened to my mom, I don't know what I would do."

She was being so much nicer about the whole thing than my so-called best friend, but Amelia was always really sensitive about things.

"So do you want to make the cookies?" she asked. "If they taste all right, you can bring some home to your mom."

"Sure," I said.

Amelia went to the pantry to get the ingredients. We had to use cornstarch and rice flour instead of regular flour, along with something called xanthan gum, which is not like regular gum at all. It's white and powdery. Luckily, Amelia can eat sugar and regular chocolate chips. We mixed everything together and each tasted a spoonful of batter before we pulled out the cookie sheet and scooped out thirty-four little blobs. "I hope these come out okay," Amelia said.

"I'm sure they will," I said. "The batter tasted really good." I was surprised at how good it was, actually. It didn't have that strange denseness that some of her food does.

Just then the phone rang. We both had cookie batter all over our fingers. Amelia went to wash her hands. The answering machine picked up before she had time to dry them and get to the phone: *"You've reached the*

Sarsen family—Susan, Stuart, Amelia, and Billy. Please leave a message following the tone, and the designated Sarsen will be delighted to return your call." It was Amelia's dad's voice on the message, except for the part when they listed their names—then they said their own names. The machine clicked, and then I heard my mom's voice. "Uh, hello, Sarsen family, this is Leigh Wheeler. I think Carly may have headed to your house. If so, can you please ask her to—"

Amelia grabbed the receiver. "Hello?" she said.

The machine hadn't turned off, so I heard Mom say, "Hi, Amelia. How are you?" I listened to them talk for a few seconds. Amelia told Mom that I was with her. I wiped my hands with a paper towel and took the phone.

"Hi, Mom," I said.

"Carly," Mom said, "I had no idea where you were."

"I just came across the street," I said. "I left you a note." I looked at Amelia and shrugged, as if to say, *You know mothers*. Amelia nodded.

"I didn't see it," Mom said. "And the note is really beside the point. You need to ask me before you disappear. I'm still your mother."

My cheeks flushed, because the answering machine was still on, and Amelia could hear the whole conversation. It was the first time Mom had gotten mad at me since she was arrested. I wanted to tell her she wasn't allowed to. I mean, how could she tell me what to do anymore? She was the one who had broken the law. Amelia turned away from me then, I guess to give me privacy.

"I want you home in the next five minutes, okay?" Mom said.

"But we just started making cookies," I said.

"I mean, it, Carly. I need to talk to you."

"Fine," I said. I hung up the phone, and Amelia turned around. "I guess I should go," I said.

"I hope you're not in trouble," she said.

"No, my mom is," I said.

Amelia was quiet for a couple seconds. "So," she said finally, "I'll drop some of the cookies off later, if you want. I'll taste them first to make sure they're not awful. But if they're good, you should have some. You did half the baking after all."

"Thanks," I said.

I put my coat back on and headed across the street. There was our house, right in the row of other houses, looking the way it always had. There were flower beds in the front yard, empty for the winter, and the steps leading up to the porch. Whenever I'm dressed up to go anywhere, Mom makes me stand on the steps to pose for a picture. Anyone looking at the house would think a nice, normal family lived in it.

I could see Mom waiting at the window in the living room, like she used to do when I was a little girl. I stepped onto the porch, and she opened the front door. "What happened today?" she asked.

"Nothing," I said. "I just felt like going to Amelia's house. You don't have to punish me or anything."

"I'm not going to," Mom said. "I'm hoping you and I can declare a truce."

I shrugged my shoulders. "Whatever," I said.

"I was thinking we could go to the mall," Mom said.

I couldn't think of a worse idea. Mom hadn't even wanted to go out in public since she was arrested. Someone might say something. If they saw us shopping in a mall, they would probably think Mom was buying things illegally, with the *Lovelock Falls* credit card. Maybe they would even be right. "I really don't think we should," I said.

"We don't have to go around here," Mom said, as if she were reading my mind. "There's a mall in New Jersey. I wanted to get you a couple bras."

I folded my arms across my chest. The sad truth was that I had no need for any bras. And even if I did, I didn't want to spend the day shopping for them with my mother. Shopping with Mom used to be one of my favorite things to do, but I would probably never want to do it again.

"No," I said.

"Are you sure?" Mom asked.

"I'm positive," I said.

"All right," she said. "Let me know if you change your mind. We can always go tomorrow."

"I won't change my mind," I told her.

Mom sighed. "Faux Pa called," she said. "Justin lost his game. They were going to stop for a bite and come home."

"I'll wait for them out here," I said.

"They'll be a little while," Mom said. "It's cold out. Faux Pa said the *Farmer's Almanac* predicts a rough winter this year."

"I don't care," I told her.

"You hate the cold," Mom said.

"I changed my mind about it," I told her. "I've changed my mind about a lot of things." I took a step back from her. I felt like I was watching myself from a distance instead of actually being in the conversation. I didn't feel like myself. This wasn't the way I usually was around my mom. Annie was the moody one. My mom and I were friends, except now we weren't.

"Listen, Carly," Mom said. "Faux Pa and I made a decision last night, and I want to tell to you about it. I was hoping to talk to you before everyone came home."

"I'm really not in the mood to talk right now," I said.

"Honey, please," Mom said. "I know it's been hard lately, but I don't want it to ruin our relationship. Things are hard enough."

"That's not my fault," I said.

"Of course it's not," Mom said. "But you have to understand this is difficult for me, too. And I never did anything to hurt you. It had nothing to do with you. You know how much I love you, right?"

I shrugged.

"Of course you don't," Mom said. "You can't—not until you have children of your own. But I love you so much. I love you more than I've ever loved anything."

There was a Carly Simon song Mom used to sing to me, "Love of My Life." Mom said Carly wrote it for her own kids. She said she felt the exact same way. I wondered if it was really true. There was a part of me that thought maybe it had all happened because she didn't love me enough. It just seemed like if you really loved your daughter, you wouldn't do anything so awful that it would ruin everything. I stared at Mom, and for a second it was like I caught a glimpse of the mom she used to be—pretty, fun, cool. I missed her so much. I missed her, and she wasn't even gone yet. "Mom?"

"Yes, honey?" Suddenly, she looked different again, more like the new version of Mom—stressed out, the lines on her face a bit deeper. It was like those pictures on the windowsill in Grandma's room at the nursing home, and how they seemed like pictures of a completely different person.

I shook my head. Mom looked like she might start to cry. "I know you're angry," she said. "I know you hate me right now. That's the worst punishment in the world." Her voice caught, and she took a deep breath. "I'm changing my plea to guilty. That way none of us will have to go through a trial—you and Faux Pa especially. Dale Addie talked to the prosecutor, and he's going to recommend the lower end of the sentencing guidelines to the judge. Do you understand what that means?"

I nodded. The lower end of the guidelines was twelve months—I remembered that from the meeting at the lawyers' office. My mother would be gone for a year.

"Let's use this time together," she said. "Let's be together." We stared at each other for a few seconds, and then Mom started to smile. "Come on," she said. "When I go away, I'll bring you back a shirt that says 'My Mom Went to Prison and All I Got Was This Lousy T-Shirt.'"

"That's not even funny," I said. I turned away from her, finally, and sat down on the front step. I could feel the cold through my jeans, but I pretended not to care. Behind me I heard the door close, and I knew she had gone back inside.

chapter thirteen

On the day Mom changed her plea to guilty, she came downstairs looking better than she had in weeks. She was wearing a white blouse tucked into a black skirt that stopped just below her knees, along with sheer black stockings and black shoes.

The funny thing was that Mom never let any of the actresses on *Lovelock Falls* wear stockings. She thought they were old-fashioned, and one of her big pet peeves was when she saw women wearing them with open-toed shoes—she hated when you could see the stocking seams.

Mom's shoes were closed-toe, so the seams weren't a problem. She looked polished and professional, as if she were going to work in an office. But it was more than that too. Her skin was smoother. The lines around her mouth and eyes were fainter and her eyes a bit brighter. It was the way her face used to be. I realized it was the makeup—she had powdered her cheeks, lined her eyes, and used blush and mascara. She looked like my old mom—the one I knew before any of this had happened. It was strange that she could still look like that.

Faux Pa came in looking the way he always does—handsome and slightly disheveled. He opened one of the kitchen cabinets and took out a coffee mug. I watched him pour himself a cup of coffee, then add in a splash of milk and some sugar. Clouds in his coffee. That's a line from Carly Simon's most famous song, by the way. She sings that dreams are like clouds in her coffee. Sometimes Mom and I try to figure out what it means, and one of our theories is that the clouds are the milk and sugar added in. You see the puff of white when you first pour the milk in, and then it fades away, like dreams do sometimes. "What time do you have to be there?" I asked him.

"The hearing is at noon," Faux Pa told me. "We're meeting with the lawyers before that, but I can still drop you off at school."

I had asked Mom and Faux Pa about going to the courthouse with them—that's where Mom had to go to change her plea. She had to stand up in front of the judge so it would be official. But they both said I should go to school instead. It's not like I really wanted to be there; I just had this fear that once Mom pled guilty, I wouldn't see her again—like the FBI agents would swoop in and arrest her right there, and haul her off to prison for the next twelve to eighteen months, or maybe even longer. In my head I pictured the same FBI agents who had come to our door that day, Special Agent Dixon Smith and Special Agent Marisa Valdez. I would probably remember their names and their faces for the rest of my life. I imagined Agent Smith handcuffing Mom and Agent Valdez (she would always be Cruella to me) standing there, smiling as she watched the whole thing.

The lawyers had said that wouldn't happen. They told Mom and Faux Pa exactly how everything would work, and Faux Pa explained it to me: The judge, the Honorable Barry J. Thompson, would be at the front of the courtroom, just the way you see on TV. The desk on a pedestal that the judge sits at is called the bench. Facing Judge Thompson would be two tables—on the left the table where the prosecutor would sit, on the right the table where Mom and her lawyers would sit. The judge would ask Mom to stand up. He'd read the charges and make sure Mom understood exactly what it meant to plead guilty—that she'd be giving up her right to a trial with a jury, and that she'd be sentenced accordingly. Then he would say, "How do you plead?" And Mom would say, "Guilty."

After that, a sentencing date would be set. Mom couldn't be sentenced until the prosecutor wrote up something called a presentence report, which would basically outline all the stuff Mom had done and what the prosecutor thought Mom's punishment should be. Mom's attorneys would read the report and write their own memo to the judge, about what a good person Mom was and how this was the first time she ever did anything against the law, so the judge should go easy on her. Judge Thompson would read all of it before deciding what Mom's sentence would be. In the meantime she'd get to come home.

"This coffee is terrible," Faux Pa said. He went to the

sink and turned his mug over, spilling the rest of the coffee out. "I think the milk is sour."

"Do you want me to make you another cup?" Mom asked.

"How can you make me another cup if we only have sour milk?" Faux Pa asked. The way he said it, you knew he wasn't really expecting Mom to answer him. She walked over to the sink. Faux Pa stepped away from her. She picked up his empty coffee mug and turned on the faucet to rinse it out. Then she put it in the dishwasher. It's always seemed silly to me to rinse the dishes off before you put them in the dishwasher. Isn't that the whole point of a dishwasher?

"Are you ready to go?" Faux Pa asked me.

"Almost," I said. "I just have to get my English book from upstairs." I stood up and brought my plate to the sink—I hadn't finished my waffle, but I wasn't really hungry. I went up to my room and grabbed *My Antonia* from my desk. I was only two chapters away from the end. When our class had originally started reading it, Mom hadn't even been arrested yet. The next book on our reading list was *The Outsiders*. I knew that by the time I finished that one, Mom might already be in prison.

I met Faux Pa in the front hall. I stuffed the book into my backpack, and he held my coat out to me. "Thanks," I said. I wondered if I should go into the kitchen to say good-bye to Mom, but she walked into the front hall right then. I dropped my bag on the stairs and put my purple coat on. Mom was watching me, and I felt strangely self-conscious about the whole thing. "I'll see you when you get home," she said.

"Okay," I said.

The edges of her lips curled. "Aren't you going to tell me to break a leg?" she asked.

"Huh?" I said.

"It's what you tell someone for good luck before a performance," she said.

"Yeah, but you don't have a performance," I reminded her.

"I know," she said. Her mouth was set straight again, no smile. "I was just kidding."

"Come on, honey," Faux Pa said to me. "We have to get going." He picked up my backpack and walked to the door. He didn't even say good-bye to Mom. He used to kiss her good-bye whenever he left the house, just a quick peck, even when he was just leaving for a few minutes. Justin always hated to see him do it. He would say, "Get a room." I have to admit that I never really liked watching my parents kiss either, but now I missed it. It felt like the family was breaking up. Most kids don't get to see their parents falling in love, but I did. I remember seeing Mom get dressed up for their dates, and when Faux Pa moved in, and of course their wedding day. Now I felt like I was seeing them fall out of love—at least seeing Faux Pa fall out of love with Mom. I knew why it was happening, but it was still an awful thing to see.

I followed Faux Pa, but just before I got to the door, I turned around and waved to Mom. Her eyes had that shiny glaze. I knew that if she started to cry right then, her makeup would get ruined. She'd have to go back upstairs and fix it. There was a part of me that wanted to go up and hug her, but I just couldn't. It was like I didn't know how to touch her in that way anymore.

"Bye," I said.

Faux Pa dropped me off in front of Preston Day. I watched him drive off in his gray car, and then I headed inside.

The day passed as if it were any other Tuesday—I had two classes, then a study hall, then one more class, and then it was time for lunch. Lauren came up to me as I was stuffing my Pre-Algebra textbook into my locker and grabbing my pea coat.

"Annie's holding the table," she said. "We can walk over together."

"What table?" I said.

"At the diner," Lauren said. "You know, she has a fourth period study hall, so she ran over to get a table before the crowd."

"I didn't know we were going to the diner today," I said.

"She wants to show us the sample invitations," Lauren said. "I thought she called everyone last night."

"She didn't call me," I said.

There was a moment when we realized what had happened—that Annie had invited Lauren, and probably Jordan, but not me. Everything seemed to stand still for an instant. I knew I wasn't being paranoid, no matter what Annie said.

Lauren started talking quickly to cover it up. "I'm sure it was just an oversight." But she and I both knew it probably wasn't one.

I shook my head. "I saw her second period in American Government, and she didn't say anything about it. She's been weird to me ever since this stuff with my mom started."

"It'll be okay," Lauren said. "I know your mom didn't do all those things. When they can't prove her guilty, there will be articles in the newspaper about that, and everything will go back to normal. You'll see."

My cheeks flushed. "I hope so," I said, even though she was obviously totally wrong. I guess I could've told her what Mom was doing right then. It wasn't exactly going to be a secret anymore. The lawyers said that the guilty plea would be a public record, which meant the reporters would find out about it. Faux Pa had even told Jessa and Justin the truth over the weekend—that Mom was really guilty, and she was going to change her plea. It was strange that Lauren and I were standing at my locker at the exact same moment that Mom was in a courtroom, in front of Judge Thompson, admitting what she had done.

I was so mad at Mom right then, because I knew things wouldn't go back to normal. The newspapers would have articles about her guilty plea. Annie would still take it out on me, and it wasn't fair. *I* hadn't done anything wrong; *I* was still the same person I always had been. I wondered if I would end up losing all my friends.

"Hey, you guys," someone called. I turned, and there was Jordan at the end of the hall. "Hurry up," she said. "Annie will be annoyed if we're too late."

"You should go," I told Lauren.

"Come with us," Lauren said. "Even Jordan just expected that you would be coming. If Annie makes a big deal about it, I'll say that I invited you. She didn't tell me *not* to invite you. Besides, you belong there."

"It's okay," I said. "I would feel too weird."

Lauren bit her bottom lip. It's her one bad habit.

Whenever she's thinking about something, she chews on her lips. They're usually pretty chapped.

"Jordan's waiting for you," I reminded her.

"I know," she said. "But I was just thinking, what if we just have lunch together—you know, the two of us?"

"You don't have to do that," I said.

"I don't mind," Lauren said. "Just give me a sec." She jogged down the hall to Jordan. I could see her lips moving, but I couldn't tell what she was saying; she was speaking too softly. I know some people claim that they can read lips, but I can't. Jordan waved to me, and Lauren came back down the hall.

"What did you tell her?" I asked.

"I said you were stressed out about Pre-Algebra and I was going to help you."

"Oh," I said.

"I would've said *I* was stressed out and *you* were helping *me*, but, you know, I didn't think that would work." I knew what she meant—no one would believe that Lauren needed help with her schoolwork. Besides, she had finished Pre-Algebra in the sixth grade.

"Are you sure this is okay?" I asked.

"Of course I'm sure," Lauren said. "Annie doesn't need me to plan her party anyway. Where do you want to go?"

"Wherever you want," I said. "It's probably too late to get a table at Slice of Life."

"We can get a couple slices to go and bring them back to the cafeteria," Lauren said. "There're always tables there."

"Okay," I said. "Thanks."

"No problem," she said.

Slice of Life was packed when Lauren and I got

there. I saw Molly Anders and Jill Galin in a booth with a couple of other eighth graders. Alex Jedder and his friends were at the table across from them. Lauren and I gave our order to the guy behind the counter. "To stay or to go?" the guy behind the counter asked.

It was a really dumb question, since there wasn't any place for us to sit. "To go," I said.

He pulled a little pizza box down from a pile on top of the oven and put our slices inside. I took the box with the pizza, and Lauren took the bag with our sodas in it. We passed Alex's table as we walked toward the door. There were three of them sitting there—this kid Nate Waxman was next to Alex, and Trevor Christopher was across from them. "Hey," Alex said. "Leaving already?"

"Yup," I said. "There aren't any tables left."

"We can make room," Alex said. "Hey, Nate, scoot over."

I was about to say no—not like it was impossible. We'd all squeezed into booths before. "Thanks," Lauren said.

I sat down next to Alex so Lauren could have the side with more room, even though I realized that Alex probably wanted to sit next to Lauren and not me. Lauren handed me my soda, and I flipped open the box of pizza. It was extra greasy. Ordinarily I would've mopped up the extra grease with napkins, but that seemed like a gross thing to do in front of the boys. I picked up my slice, took a bite, and burned the roof of my mouth.

"So my brother got me this book," Trevor said. "It's called *Would You Rather*, and you have to choose, like would you rather take a bath in elephant pee or drink a cup of spit."

I couldn't believe I'd been worried about a couple of greasy napkins. "I think we're grossing out Carly and Lauren," Alex said.

"It's okay," Lauren said. "I have an older brother, so I've been desensitized."

Trevor went on about the things in the book—licking the bottom of your shoe versus picking up dog poo with your hands, being trapped in an elevator with someone who has incredibly bad breath or with a swarm of bees. Lauren and I played along. It was funny, because lunch with the boys was so completely different from lunch with just girls. They were loud, they punched each other in the arm, and they talked with food in their mouths. But I didn't mind, because I was having fun. Being around the boys made me feel like a teenager. I thought about how Annie was inviting the boys to her party, and I understood completely why she wanted to.

But then remembering Annie made me feel upset all over again. She was planning her birthday party without me. I came up with the theme for the party, and she was leaving me out! It made me glad that Alex liked Lauren and not Annie. Maybe that made me a bad friend, but Annie had been a bad friend to me first.

The boys started talking about the cars they wanted to drive when they got their licenses: Alex wanted a Ferrari, Nate said a Lamborghini, and Trevor picked a Porsche. It reminded me of Justin and his video games—he played this race car game called Need for Speed, and he was always talking about which cars were faster, and how many points he needed to be able to use the fastest car.

"If you're getting a black one, it has to be without a

racing stripe," Lauren said. "Otherwise it would look too skunklike."

Alex laughed again. "Hey dudes—and dudettes," Nate said, "we better get going. We've got, like, five minutes before fifth period."

I looked up at the clock on the wall. Time had passed more quickly than I'd realized. Mom's court hearing was probably over too. I wondered if everything had happened the way it was supposed to. I didn't even know what the Honorable Barry J. Thompson looked like, and he would be the one deciding what would happen to Mom.

"Thanks for letting us join you guys," Lauren said.

"No problem," Alex said. "You and Carly can crash our table anytime."

Lauren looked at me and smiled. "Thanks," she said. "Maybe we will again someday."

chapter fourteen

The next morning there was another article by Christine Barrett in the newspaper:

> **Ex-*Lovelock Falls* staffer Leigh Wheeler pled guilty to felony embezzlement and conspiracy to commit embezzlement on Tuesday. Sentencing is set for next month, when Wheeler will likely be sent to a minimum-security facility. Wheeler declined our request for comment, but sources close to the family say she is getting her affairs in order.**

I could feel my heart thump-thumping as I read that last line. "Getting her affairs in order"—because of course that was what people were supposed to do when they knew they were about to die. Last year this girl Bethany Sorren's father died. Bethany is a year below me at Preston. There was a memorial service that Mom and I went to, which was incredibly sad. Bethany's mom gave a speech about what a wonderful man her husband had been. When the service was over, Mom went up to Bethany's mother and gave her a hug, even though they really didn't know each other. Afterward I'd said to Mom, "You must know what she's going through." Mom said, "Yes, I do. But at least Cliff Sorren had time to get his affairs in order. With your dad it was so sudden. I had to figure it all out myself."

I read the sentence over again. I guess being sent to prison is like dying, at least in a temporary way—you leave your family, and they have to go on without you.

Christine Barrett's article went on for a few more paragraphs, basically recapping what Mom's crimes were, and that sources at *Lovelock Falls* said that everyone was "shocked" to learn what Mom and Vivette had been doing. I wondered who all those sources of Christine Barrett's were. She didn't mention anyone by name. I decided that anonymous sources shouldn't be allowed. It was like being at school and gossiping behind people's backs. It was completely immature and mean.

I don't know if Mom saw the newspaper. She was still in her room when Faux Pa took me to school. She didn't have to wake up by a certain time. She didn't have anywhere to go. It must have been so weird, to just be waiting around the house with nothing to do until the sentencing. That was it. She had pled guilty. There was no going back, like Dale said.

Faux Pa told me to have a good day at school and to try not to let everything that was going on with

Mom affect my work. I knew that would be impossible. How was I going to concentrate? People were going to know. It would be worse than when she was arrested, because now I couldn't even pretend that it was all a misunderstanding.

I walked across the parking lot toward the building, passing Maggie Newell, a girl in my English class. We'd never really been friends, so I guess it wasn't a big deal that she didn't say hello to me, but I couldn't help but wonder if she was trying to avoid me because she knew about Mom. I imagined her sitting at the table in her kitchen that morning—I'd been to Maggie's house for a birthday party in second grade, and I knew exactly what the kitchen looked like. There was wallpaper with cartoon cows, cows sitting up, cows upside down, cows seemingly flying. If you ask me, it looked like it should be wallpaper in a kid's bedroom. I mean, what do cartoon cows have to do with a kitchen? Maybe because you can eat cow, but that's kind of a gross reason. Anyway, I imagined Maggie sitting there in the cow-filled kitchen, eating a bowl of cereal, and her parents across the table, drinking coffee and thumbing through different sections of the paper. "Hey, look at this," her dad would've said. "It looks like Carly Wheeler's mother is in even more trouble now."

I wondered how many kids at Preston had the newspaper delivered to their house each morning. How many of their parents read Christine Barrett's article? How many of them already knew? It's weird to have people knowing things about your life before you even tell them yourself. If I had it my way, I wouldn't tell them at all. I just wouldn't invite anyone over to my house for the next twelve to eighteen months, and then as soon as Mom was back, I could pretend like she'd been there all along.

Annie was waiting for me at my locker. "I know all about what happened yesterday," she said.

She was looking at me so intensely, like she could see through me. I felt exposed, naked. "I knew you would," I said.

"Molly was at the tennis court yesterday, and she told me all about it," Annie continued. "So I guess you lied when you told Jordan you were stressed out about math."

"What?"

"Don't pretend like you don't know what I mean," Annie said. "You told Jordan that you couldn't come to lunch yesterday because you needed help with Pre-Algebra."

I was so focused on Mom that it took me a couple seconds to figure out what Annie was talking about. Then it all started coming back to me. I had been there, in front of my locker, with Lauren the day before. She'd told Jordan that we couldn't go to lunch because of me.

"If you make up another lame excuse, I won't believe you," Annie said. I didn't want to make her mad at Lauren, too, so I didn't bother mentioning that Lauren was the one who came up with the first lame excuse.

"You didn't even invite me to lunch yesterday," I told her.

"So?" Annie said. "You always come to lunch."

Maybe I was wrong about the whole thing. Maybe it had been an oversight. How could I explain to her how different everything felt right now? I didn't think she would understand.

I stood there, feeling dumb, because that's the way

Annie always makes me feel when we fight. "Lauren told me you called her Monday night to invite her to lunch. I didn't want to go if I wasn't invited."

"Whatever," Annie said. "That doesn't mean you get to lie. Molly and Jill saw you sitting next to Alex Jedder at lunch."

"That just happened," I said. "We went to Slice of Life for pizza, and Alex just happened to be there. He told us we could sit at his table because there weren't any other seats. You know how crowded it gets there."

"Come on," Annie said. "You wouldn't have lied about math unless you had something to hide. I asked you if you liked him, and you told me no. And then you guys just happened to eat together."

"Just because we had lunch doesn't mean I like him—not in that way," I said. "You know we're lab partners. I sit next to him practically every day."

"It's not the same, and you know it," Annie said.

It wasn't the same. I guess I should've told her about Alex and me being sort of friends. It would be different if Alex wasn't the cutest boy in school, or if Annie hadn't told us about her crush. "Really, lunch wasn't a big deal," I said. "I swear."

"I don't believe you," Annie said.

"I wouldn't lie," I said.

"You lied yesterday," Annie reminded me. "Just like your mom lied to us."

"My mom doesn't have anything to do with lunch," I said.

"She does," Annie insisted. "You lie just like her. Remember, we heard her in her office talking to Vivette, and she said everything was fine? My mom showed me the article this morning. I should've figured it out. She always acted different, and my mom says she's suspicious of anyone who acts so lenient."

"But you like my mom," I reminded her. "She never did anything bad to you." It's funny how I could be so mad at Mom, but when Annie started talking about her, I got so protective. She didn't have a right to say those things! After all, my mom used to do such nice things for Annie—like bringing her to the set and letting her stay at our house whenever Annie wanted. She keeps Sprite in the fridge for when Annie comes over, even though no one else likes to drink it. Besides, if anyone is too lenient, it's Mrs. Rothschild—she let Annie get a cell phone in fourth grade, and she's always buying Annie things and redoing her bedroom.

"When she drove us home from the city that day, she ran the stop sign, but she didn't think she should have to get a ticket," Annie said.

"That's not what happened at all," I said. "You were there—the police officer decided himself not to ticket her."

Annie shook her head. "You're exactly like her," she said. "My mom doesn't think I should be friends with you anymore, and I agree with her."

Annie turned to walk away. I just stood there. It wasn't true, what she said. I wasn't exactly like Mom. *My best friend hates me*, I thought. *I've lost my best friend.* I should've seen it coming by the way Annie was acting, and I guess I had known. But there's a big difference between knowing something in your head and actually having it all said to your face.

I remembered something that had happened the summer before, one night when I'd slept over at Annie's house. We were sharing Annie's bed—it's queen-size, so big enough for us both. It was really late, and Annie was already sleeping, but I couldn't fall asleep. There were noises in the hallway. I figured it was the dog. The Rothschilds have a dog, Jasper, who I sort of feel sorry for. No one pays too much attention to him. I think they just got him for decoration. He used to be a show dog before he got too old. I decided to see if Jasper was okay, and I slid out of bed as quietly as I could. I cracked open the door, but it wasn't the dog in the hallway. It was Mrs. Rothschild. She walked past me without seeming to see me. She was moving funny, bumping against the walls on her way back to her bedroom. I could tell she was drunk.

I closed the door, quickly and quietly, and climbed back into bed with Annie. She turned over and opened her eyes. "Where were you?"

"I heard Jasper in the hall," I lied.

"Oh," Annie said sleepily. She turned back over, and after a few minutes her breaths became deeper again. For some reason my heart was racing. I knew Annie would've been really upset if she'd known her mom had been like that. I never told anyone about it. I never even told Annie.

But I wanted to tell her about it now. I knew it was mean, but I wanted her to feel as bad and embarrassed as I did. I wanted her to know that her mom made mistakes too. I felt frozen. I just stood there as Annie disappeared around the corner.

chapter fifteen

For as long as I can remember, my family has had this cheesy Thanksgiving tradition of going around the table and saying what we're thankful for. Every year I rolled my eyes along with Jessa and Justin whenever it was time to do it, but secretly I sort of liked it. It was nice to think of all the good things I had around me—my parents, my friends, the three-cheese potatoes.

But this time around I wasn't feeling at all thankful on Thanksgiving. My mom was a criminal, and my best friend hated me. I thought there should be a special holiday for people whose lives aren't so great—the Un-Thanksgiving. We could each make a list of things that sucked.

Of course I didn't suggest it. I just sat at the table, in my seat next to Mom. That was always my seat when we all had dinner. Jessa was across from me, and Justin was next to her. Faux Pa sat at the head of the table, in between Mom and Justin. We didn't need to put the extra leaf in the table, because Vivette and Ed weren't there. I would never have three-cheese potatoes again. I wondered if Vivette had made them anyway. What were they doing for the holiday? Was Ed mad at Vivette? Had he left her? Or maybe he'd known about it all along. Did they go to another friend's house and act like none of this was even happening?

Mom and Faux Pa must have decided we didn't need to go around the table and say what we were thankful for, because when we sat down Faux Pa just started carving the turkey.

"Justin, white meat, right?" Faux Pa asked.

"No, dark meat," Justin said. "I want a leg."

"I'm the one who likes white meat," Jessa said.

"Right," Faux Pa said. He sounded distracted. "I'm sorry. What about you, Carly?"

"I don't care," I said. The truth is, I'm not that crazy about turkey. Faux Pa gave me a slice of white meat and a slice of dark meat. Mom passed around the cranberry sauce, which I hate because it's too slimy, and green-bean casserole, which I like because Mom puts cheese in it. When I was little, Mom thought I was a picky eater—but that was before she met Justin. I poured an extra amount of gravy on the turkey so it wouldn't taste too bad. The night didn't feel special at all, like it could've been any night and not the fourth Thursday in November.

"The turkey's a little dry," Mom said.

"It's fine, Leigh," Faux Pa said.

"I'm sorry," Mom said. "I'm not doing anything right lately."

Faux Pa didn't say anything to correct her. I guess he

agreed. The phone rang, and Justin jumped up. "I'll get it," he said.

"No," Faux Pa said. "We're eating."

"But it might be Mom calling to say Happy Thanksgiving," Justin said. He was racing back toward the kitchen to get the phone.

"Check the caller ID first," Faux Pa warned, but I knew Justin wasn't paying attention.

"Hello?" I heard Justin say. He came back into the dining room carrying the phone. "It's not Mom," he reported. "It's for Leigh."

Mom hadn't really been talking on the phone much, except to Dale and Jamie. Justin held the phone out to her, and for a second she just looked at it like she didn't know what to do. But then she took it from him. She looked at the little screen to check the caller ID, and then she pressed the receiver against her ear. "Hi," she said. There was a pause for a couple seconds. "Of course I am," Mom said. We were all looking at her, and I guess she noticed right then, because she stood up and walked into the kitchen.

"Who was calling?" Faux Pa asked.

"I don't know," Justin said. "Some woman."

"I hate phone calls at dinner, and Leigh knows it," Faux Pa said. "Who would call on Thanksgiving anyway?" He asked the question more to himself than to any of us, but Jessa answered him anyway.

"It doesn't feel like Thanksgiving in here," she said. "It feels like a funeral." I glanced up at Jessa, who was dressed in black, as usual. She's always ready for a funeral. "Sorry, Carly," Jessa said. "You could've come to my aunt Barbara's with us. That's where my mom went."

Barbara is one of Jocelyn's sisters. Jessa and Justin

are related to all of these people I don't even know. It made me feel like I didn't even belong there with them, even though I was sitting in my own house.

"That's enough, Jessa," Faux Pa said. "It was my year to have Thanksgiving with you, and we're making the best of things."

"I don't want to go to Aunt Barbara's anyway," Justin said. "Mom never lets me eat the drumstick, because white meat is healthier."

"Maybe I'll tell her you ate it," Jessa said.

"Oh, come on, kids," Faux Pa said. "Not today."

"I was just kidding," Jessa said, but somehow I doubted she really was.

Mom came back into the dining room, her eyes shining. She blinked quickly. "What was that about?" Faux Pa asked.

"Nothing," Mom said. "Vivette called to wish us a happy Thanksgiving."

Faux Pa's face turned red. "That woman should be in jail," he said. *Prison,* I thought. *Jail is a short-term facility. Prison is long-term.* "We discussed this, Leigh. You can't talk to her."

"It really doesn't matter anymore, Jon," Mom said. "I took a plea, and she took a plea. But I told her I had to go."

"Vivette pled guilty?" I asked.

"Yes," Mom said.

"How long is she going away for?"

"She hasn't been sentenced yet," Mom told me.

"But how long do they think?"

"I don't know," Mom said. "I didn't talk to her that long." I wondered whether she and Vivette would be sent to the same place. Maybe they would be roommates in a cell. Faux Pa wouldn't be happy about that.

"Sit down now, Leigh," Faux Pa said. He was speaking like Mom was a little kid.

"I'm not hungry anymore," Mom said. "I'm going to go up to my room."

"Great," Faux Pa said. "Abandon your family on Thanksgiving." I wondered if he was really thinking about how Mom would be abandoning us to go to prison.

"This is hard for me too," Mom said. Her voice cracked, and she didn't even try to make a joke. Instead she turned and walked out of the room. We were all quiet after that. Around me were the sounds of forks and knives scraping against the good dishes—the ones we don't eat off of at regular meals. Suddenly someone burped. "Justin!" Jessa said.

"Say 'excuse me,'" Faux Pa said.

"Excuse me," Justin said. Usually Justin starts laughing when he does something gross like burp or fart, but he didn't even smile. Everyone was quiet again. It was probably the most uncomfortable meal I'd ever sat through, and it felt like it was taking me an extra-long time to chew and swallow each bite. Even with the gravy, the turkey was too dry. I pushed it aside and just ate the green beans.

Finally, dinner was over. I stood up and helped clear the table. We piled the dishes in the sink and the left-over food on the counter, but we didn't put anything away. Faux Pa went into the den to watch a movie, Justin went to play video games on the computer, and Jessa went up to her room, probably to read. I didn't know what to do with myself. I guess I could've cleaned up the kitchen, but that didn't seem fair at all. Usually after Thanksgiving dinner was over, we all sat at the table for a little while and just talked. *This time last year, we ate brownies and played Catch Phrase,* I thought to myself. *This time next year, Mom will probably be eating Thanksgiving dinner in prison.* Part of me thought I should go upstairs and just be with her, because pretty soon I wouldn't get to see her at all. I should soak her up and spend extra time with her to make up for all the time she would be gone. But I didn't want to be with her right then.

I went up to my room to be by myself. I never used to be the kind of person who shut herself up in her room. I really wished I had a TV in there—Faux Pa and Mom have a rule about no televisions in the kids' rooms. I think it's really dumb. I mean, I guess I can understand it for little kids, so they don't end up turning it on themselves and watching shows that are too mature for them, but I don't get it for someone my age.

I read part of an old book instead, my favorite book—*Bridge to Terabithia*—where this kid has a best friend who dies. I'd already read it about a hundred times, so I knew exactly what was going to happen. It made me cry in the same places it always did. At least no one close to me was dying. I should be thankful for things like that. But this really messed-up part of me felt like maybe that would be easier—if Mom were dying, people would feel sorry for me, and they'd gather around me. Annie would still want to be my friend. I imagined the whole disastrous thing in my head. I knew it was an awful thing to think about.

I put the book away and got into bed, even though I wasn't really tired. I turned out the light and just lay there for a long time. I couldn't get comfortable. It was really dark in my room, so I couldn't even watch the dust particles. Time passed. Everyone else was probably sleeping, or at least lying silently in their own beds.

Down the hall a door opened. I stayed still and tried to figure out who was walking down the hall by the sound of the footsteps—definitely not Justin, because the steps were too light. He tends to pound the ground as he walks, as if a walk down the hall is some sort of race. I assumed Faux Pa was sleeping downstairs, so it was probably Mom or Jessa. For some reason I was nervous. I couldn't tell you why, but my heart was beating a little faster. I listened to whoever it was walk down the hall toward the stairs. After a few seconds I thought I heard the front door open and close. Where would anyone have to go in the middle of the night?

I guess you would leave in the middle of the night if you wanted to run away. It would be the best time to do it—no one would see you, and you wouldn't have to have any long, drawn-out good-byes. My heart was pounding now. Criminals ran away to escape having to go to prison. There were sometimes stories about it on the news. They went to Mexico and Canada and places like that, and their families never saw them again. I lay there in my bed, my whole body shaking. I wondered if I should get up and run after Mom. I didn't know what to do, and the more time passed, the more I knew it was too late.

chapter sixteen

The next morning the kitchen was completely spotless. Mom must've gone downstairs to clean it up. Maybe she'd opened the front door last night to put the garbage out. I didn't ask her. She hadn't run away, and it didn't even seem to matter anymore. She'd boxed up some of the leftover food to bring to my grandmother in the nursing home.

Grandma used to get upset that we didn't visit her on Thanksgiving itself. The nursing home makes a special dinner for all of the residents, and Grandma would complain that it tasted bad and reminded her that she was all alone. But she isn't really aware of the days of the week anymore, so she doesn't realize that we're coming a day late. In fact she doesn't even realize that it's Thanksgiving at all. Mom had called ahead to tell the nursing home not to feed her lunch, and we brought over the food. It seemed like a long time since

Mom and I had done anything together. We didn't talk about what a disaster Thanksgiving dinner had been. She parked in the parking lot. We got out of the car and grabbed the bags from the backseat.

The nursing home is a big brick building next to the Hudson River. When Grandma first moved into it, Mom made a big deal out of making sure she had a room that faced the water. But it doesn't really matter, because Grandma likes the shades drawn. Otherwise, Grandma explains, there's a glare and she can't see the TV. Basically, that's what she does all day long—she lies in bed and watches TV. When we come to visit, Mom turns the volume on the TV down a little bit, but Grandma won't let her turn it off all the way.

Grandma lives on the third floor, in a room about the size of my bedroom. She used to have a big house, but it was sold along with most of the stuff inside it. Now everything she owns is in her room at the nursing home. This is what she has: a bed, a couple of chairs for guests, a dresser, a bookshelf, some pictures, and about two dozen little elephant statues. She used to collect elephants. In her old house there were about a hundred of them, but they wouldn't all fit in her room at the nursing home. Mom brought some of them home to our house. The pink one that was always my favorite is in my bedroom now. I think it's made of quartz, and it's heavy, like a paperweight. The ones Grandma kept are turned so their trunks all face the window, because supposedly that's lucky. But since the shades are always drawn, I wonder if it counts.

We got off the elevator and walked down the hall to Grandma's room. A few of the residents were out in the hallway, just sitting there in their wheelchairs, like they were waiting for something—I don't know what. Sometimes when I walk down the hall at the nursing home, I feel like I'm doing something wrong. The residents look so old and so sad, and it's like I shouldn't be looking at them sitting there; it's too private.

The door to Grandma's room was open. "Hi, Mother," Mom said as we walked in. It's always weird to hear Mom say "Mother," since I don't usually think of her as a daughter. "Happy Thanksgiving." She had to talk extra loud, because the TV was blaring. We put down the food, took our jackets off, and draped them across the back of one of the guest chairs. Mom picked up the remote to turn the volume on the TV down.

"Don't turn it off," Grandma said, the way she always did. "I can't miss anything." There was a commercial for a vacuum cleaner on the TV right then. I knew it wasn't anything Grandma would ever need. The nursing home had a staff that cleaned the rooms for the residents.

"Don't worry, Mother," Mom said. "I'm just making the volume lower."

"Who is that with you?" Grandma asked.

"It's Carly," Mom told her. "Your granddaughter."

"I don't know her," Grandma said.

It used to be that Mom would remind Grandma who I was and then she would recognize me, like a lightbulb went on inside her, but now she had forgotten me completely. It's because she has Alzheimer's disease, and it gets worse as time goes on. When I was younger, I thought it was called *Old Timer's* disease—because it's a disease old people sometimes get, when they forget a lot of things. It's more than that, really; they lose their whole personality. Mom says I can't take

Grandma's forgetting me personally, because it's the disease and it doesn't have anything to do with me. But it's hard not to feel uncomfortable when your own grandmother doesn't know who you are. Sometimes Mom jokes that at least Grandma has forgotten all the bad things, but it just makes me scared to think about losing everything like that. It's hard for me to remember Grandma the way she used to be. Mom says she had a really sharp mind. She was good at crossword puzzles, and she loved talking about politics. But I can't remember things like that. I'm losing my memories too.

Grandma was looking at me like I was a stranger. I started to wonder where memories go—like, do they disappear completely? Is there a heaven for memories? Or maybe they were trapped somewhere inside her, like in a prison, and she couldn't get to them anymore.

"Of course you know Carly," Mom said. She took one of the pictures off the windowsill, the picture of Grandma holding me the day I was born. "See, here you are together," Mom said, tapping the glass on the frame. "Remember this day? You stayed at the hospital the entire time. My labor was eighteen hours, and you wouldn't leave until the baby was born."

Grandma leaned over toward the picture Mom was holding. In it her hair was brown instead of gray. Her eyelids weren't strangely thick and red-rimmed. None of the bad stuff had happened, and she looked like a completely different person. "That's not me," Grandma said. "I don't know these people."

She lay back on the bed, and Mom put the picture back on the windowsill. "We brought you lunch," Mom said. "Turkey and cranberry sauce."

"What about Fritos?"

One of the things Grandma still remembers is how much she likes Fritos. The best present you can give her is one of those jumbo bags. One time Mom bought Doritos instead of Fritos, and Grandma went nuts. She practically had a tantrum, like a little kid. "We have Fritos, too," Mom said. "For dessert."

"The boys came in on horseback last night," Grandma said. "I've always loved palominos."

That's just how it is to talk to Grandma—she has a tendency to say things that don't really make sense. She mentions the boys sometimes, but we never know who they are—maybe boys from her past that she remembers, or maybe boys that she just made up. Mom says you just have to smile at the things Grandma says. But the truth is that it's just so sad, and Mom couldn't hide the fact that it made her sad, too.

The commercials ended, and the show Grandma was watching came back on. It was *Lovelock Falls*. Of course Grandma watched it, since Mom had worked there for so many years. But I hadn't seen it since that day I'd called Ally and she'd told me she didn't think we should talk until things were resolved. I probably wouldn't ever see Ally in person again.

"Why don't we turn this off and talk for a little while?" Mom asked.

"No," Grandma said. "You always have crazy ideas."

Mom looked at me. "I'm sorry," she said.

"What are you apologizing to her for?" Grandma asked. "You didn't do anything to her."

"Calm down, Mother," Mom said. "I'll set your tray up now, okay?"

"You have to," Grandma said. "I can't do it myself,

and I'm famished. You know, lunch is supposed to be before my shows. It's late today."

"We were running a little bit behind schedule," Mom said. She didn't say that the reason we were running late was because she and Faux Pa had been talking behind closed doors for half the morning. She just pulled the turkey and side dishes out of the bag, arranged them on the tray, and tucked a napkin into the collar of Grandma's shirt, just like a bib. Then she rolled the tray over so Grandma could eat in bed.

Grandma picked a piece of turkey up in her hand. She waved it toward the TV. "This girl Violet is a good girl," Grandma said. She could remember Ally's fake TV character but not her own real-life granddaughter. "She just gets herself in trouble sometimes."

Life is like a soap opera, I thought. *Except you don't always wear fancy clothes.*

And so we sat there watching *Lovelock Falls*. I recognized Ally's dress—the multicolored one with the crocheted top. The episode on TV was the one that had been filmed the day Annie and I were on the set. What were the chances of that? All of a sudden, Ally-as-Violet was leaving her ex-husband's hospital room and walking briskly down the corridor. Dr. Sparling was around the corner, talking to a couple of nurses. One of them leaned forward and brushed Dr. Sparling's cheek with her hand. Ally rounded the corner and grabbed his arm. "It will be a disaster of epic proportions," she told him. "It will change all—all the things you are."

"All the things you are," Grandma repeated in a singsong voice. "All the things you are." Then her voice cracked.

Right then Grandma seemed to understand how

everything was changing. Of course, I knew she wasn't really talking about any of the stuff that was going on in real life.

"Oh, Mother," Mom said.

"I have to go to the bathroom," Grandma said.

Mom pressed the call button on the side of Grandma's bed, and within a few seconds a nurse showed up. "Hi, Carol," Mom said.

"Hi, Leigh," Carol said. "Happy Thanksgiving."

"To you, too," Mom said. "I love the new scrubs by the way. That periwinkle is great on you."

I didn't remember the old scrubs, but it was the kind of thing Mom would notice. Carol smiled. "Thank you," she said.

"I really have to go to the bathroom," Grandma said.

"All right, Gwen," Carol said. She moved toward Grandma. For some reason I felt really scared right then, just thinking about how Grandma needed help cutting her food and going to the bathroom. "Why don't you two give us a few minutes," Carol said.

"Of course," Mom said. "We'll just be in the hallway, Mother."

I followed Mom out the door. Across the hall there was an old woman sitting in a wheelchair with a doll in her lap, cradling it like it was a real baby. I tried not to look at her, but I couldn't help looking at her. She was rocking in her seat, back and forth, back and forth. "Ho, ho, ho," she said to the doll, reminding me of Santa Claus. "Don't cry. Ho, ho, ho."

"We won't stay much longer," Mom said. I turned away from the woman and looked at Mom. "After Carol's finished with Grandma, we'll just go in and say good-bye."

"Okay," I said. I remembered how Mom had once

told me that she wanted me to visit her when she was old and in a nursing home. I didn't want to think about her ever being so helpless. I just wanted her to be a normal, healthy mom. I wanted her to be someone I could count on to take care of me.

Carol peeked her head out the door and said we could come back in. She chatted with us for a few minutes. I didn't think she knew about Mom, because she was talking like everything was normal, asking us whether we were going away for winter vacation, and saying how she was already tired of the cold weather and couldn't wait for the spring. It was nice to have a conversation like that, but I was kind of scared, too, like any minute Carol could find out the truth.

Before long Mom said it was time for us to get going. We put our jackets back on. There was still food left, so Mom decided to leave it with Grandma. Carol said she would rinse the containers so Mom could pick them up the next time she visited.

"Thank you," Mom said. "You really go beyond the call."

"So do you," Carol said. "She's lucky you come to visit so often. I have some patients whose families live far away, and some others who live close by, but they just never come."

"Bye, Mother," Mom said. "See you next time." I waved from the doorway.

"Say good-bye, Gwen," Carol prompted.

"Good-bye, Gwen," Grandma said, and she started laughing. She seemed really delighted. Mom says mood changes are a part of Alzheimer's disease, but I thought it was weird that she seemed happiest when we were leaving.

Outside, it was one of those days where the sky is really bright blue and the sun is shining, but the air is cold. Faux Pa once told me that in the winter it's actually warmer when the sky is gray and the clouds are dark and heavy, because they're like a blanket, blocking the really cold air. We got into the car, and Mom turned the dial so the heat would come on full blast.

"Grandma was quoting Carly Simon," Mom said. "Did you notice?"

"No."

"All the Things You Are," Mom said. "It wasn't just on the show—it's the name of a song. Although Carly didn't sing the original version—Grandma probably doesn't even know Carly's version. But I'm sure you've heard it."

"I don't remember," I said.

"It will be weird not to come here every week," she continued. "I don't know if Grandma will even notice."

"She knows who you are," I reminded her.

"Sometimes she does," Mom said. "Sometimes I think she's just pretending because she knows she's supposed to know me. But Faux Pa said he'll bring you here when I'm gone."

I'd never gone to visit Grandma without Mom there with me. There were moments, like right then when we were sitting in the car, when I realized how much I was going to miss Mom. I didn't know what to say.

"Dale Addie is working on my sentencing memo right now," Mom said. "You know what it is, right?"

"It's the memo they have to give to the judge before he tells you the official sentence."

"Right," Mom said. "Basically, it tells the story from my perspective, and then gives the judge other information about me—all the good stuff I've done in my life, so he doesn't just think of me as the person who made this one mistake. I've done some good things, don't you think?"

I nodded. Mom *had* done good things. She ran the charity clothing drive at Preston every Christmas. Last year one of our neighbor's dogs ran away, and Mom drove around the neighborhood for hours and hours. And she was a nice person. She always complimented people and made them feel good about themselves. She was really good at remembering people's birthdays. I used to think she was the greatest mother in the entire world.

"You're the best thing I've ever done," Mom said. "You know that, right?"

"Does that mean I'll be in the memo?" I asked.

"Yes," Mom said. "Dale said you're an important part. I raised you myself all those years, and look who you've grown up to be—you're kind, you're surrounded by friends."

Lately, I wasn't quite so surrounded by friends, but I hadn't talked to Mom about it. I used to talk to her about everything, but now she was the reason things were changing, and I didn't know how to tell her about that.

"You work hard in school," Mom continued. "Remember when you won the science award last year? I was so proud of you. When I was sitting there in the auditorium and they called your name, I thought I would just burst."

"It was just an honorable mention," I said. I wondered if it would be better for the sentencing memo if I'd won first place. Would Mom be getting less time in prison if

I had gotten a blue ribbon instead of a purple one? I didn't think so, but I should've worked harder, just in case. My project was about the factors that affect seed germination, like the amount of water, temperature, and light. I could've tested the seeds in more environments. I could have watered them with flavored water, or stuck them under different colored lights.

I felt responsible, but it really wasn't fair. After all, I had done that experiment by myself. Faux Pa had helped a little bit, but Mom hadn't at all, except for helping to carry everything into school the day I had to hand my project in. Why did she have to tell the judge about it? It was almost like she wanted to take credit for it.

"What if I don't want to be in the memo?" I asked her.

"What do you mean?"

"I didn't have anything to do with what happened at *Lovelock Falls*."

"Of course not," Mom said. "Everyone knows you didn't. But you have an awful lot to do with me."

There were things about me that had to do with Mom, but there were things about me that were just me. I felt like she was taking them away from me. And what if Annie found out that Mom was using me in the sentencing memo? She would think I had done something wrong too.

I didn't want Mom to go away for a long time. I guessed I should care more about Mom than about Annie. I was just so messed up inside. Mom reached over and put her hand on my knee. We drove the rest of the way home in silence.

chapter seventeen

The next week I got a cold, and Mom got busy with her sentencing memo. Dale and Jamie were writing it, but they had asked Mom to help with the parts about all the good things she had done. Mom went through her old files, pulling out anything she thought Jamie or Dale could use: the thank-you notes she'd received each year from the Fletcher Women and Children's Shelter (where Mom always sent the clothes from the Preston clothing drive), information about her position on the Parents' Council (even though she had resigned right after she pled guilty), and my report cards (which shouldn't have counted because they were my grades and not hers).

Tuesday night my cold got really bad. I was up coughing all night long. Faux Pa didn't want me to miss any more school, but even he had to agree that it was a good idea for me to stay home Wednesday and rest. I wrapped myself up in one of Grandma's afghans and settled myself on the couch in the den. Grandma used to knit, and we have a bunch of her afghans in the hall closet. The couch in the den is where I always stay when I'm sick, so I can watch TV and not feel trapped in my room. Of course, now whenever I thought about being trapped, I remembered how Mom would probably be heading to prison.

I lay down on the couch, sort of at an awkward angle. It's always hard to get comfortable when I have a cold. It's easiest for me to sleep with my face scrunched up against my pillow. But then I get all stuffed up and I have to blow my nose.

Mom wandered in to check on me. She had a coffee mug in her right hand and a stack of papers tucked under her left arm. She put everything down on the coffee table and walked over to the couch so she could press her palm against my forehead. "You feel pretty cool," she said.

"I don't think I have a fever," I told her.

"Good," she said. "Rest up and maybe you can go to school tomorrow."

"Yeah, maybe," I said. I couldn't decide if I would rather be at school or be at home.

Mom picked her coffee up and held the mug in her hands like she was warming them. She glanced down at the liquid inside. "You know what I was thinking this morning?"

"What?"

"Maybe Carly Simon was talking about clouds in her coffee because the morning, when you drink your coffee, is such a foggy time. You're just waking up, and your dreams are still in your head. She could've been staring into her coffee mug, with the memory of her dreams fading, trying to remember all the things she was supposed to do for the day."

I shrugged. "Maybe," I said.

"Speaking of things that have to get done," Mom said, "I should get back to this." She put the coffee down and picked up her papers.

"Is that the sentencing memo?" I asked her.

"The first draft of it," Mom said. "Jamie e-mailed it this morning."

"Do you like it? I mean, do you think it's good enough?"

"I can't tell," Mom said. "It's hard to judge when you read about yourself. Do you want to read it?"

I shook my head. "I'm too stuffed up to read," I said.

"Well maybe you can help me. Dale told me to make a list of people who can write letters on my behalf," she said.

"What for?"

"It's part of what she and Jamie will submit to the court," Mom said. "They'll attach the letters as exhibits to the sentencing memo."

"Why?"

"I guess it's not enough for Dale to just write about me being a good person—they need other people to say it, too."

It seemed like a weird thing to have to do—to call people up and say, *I know I broke the law, but can you write me a letter of recommendation?* It was like Mom was applying to college, and not about to go to prison.

"Dale said it would go a long way if I could get someone from *Lovelock Falls* to write a letter on my behalf. I called Ally last night."

Inside my chest my heart started fluttering, like a bird was flapping its wings inside me. "What did she say?"

"She said she couldn't," Mom said. She sounded defeated, but not at all surprised. "She's very angry with me right now."

"Maybe someone else from the show will write a letter," I said.

"I think it's probably too complicated for them to get involved," Mom said. "But there are other people to ask. Bob Gilles said he'd write a letter."

"I don't know who that is," I said.

"You've met Bob," Mom said. "He's the director of Grandma's nursing home."

"But he's not famous," I said.

"No, but he can write about what I've done for Grandma, and how hard it would be for her if I'm sent away for too long."

It didn't seem like it would be so hard for Grandma, since she didn't even have any sense of time. Mom herself had said Grandma might not even notice she was missing. It would be much harder for me, but I didn't say anything.

"I'm going to call Carson Rothschild this afternoon," Mom said.

"Annie's dad? Why?"

"He's got one of those names people know," Mom said. Annie's dad owns buildings—that's how he's made so much money. Sometimes we'll be in the car and pass a sign with his name on it. Faux Pa says Carson Rothschild must be an egomaniac to want his name boldly displayed on every building he owns. "He's a prominent businessman," Mom continued. "People consider him an upstanding member of the community."

"I don't think you should ask him," I said. "You barely even know him."

"I've known the Rothschilds for years," Mom said.

"But Annie heard you, remember? I thought you were worried about her getting involved."

"I've already pled guilty," Mom said. "I'm trying to do everything I can to be away as little time as possible. It's not easy to ask people for favors, but I'm doing it for you. A letter from Carson on my behalf might mean something to the judge. Maybe he'd send me away for less time. You want that, right? I know it's been hard, but don't you want your old lady around?"

Of course I wanted that. But Mom didn't know about the fight I'd had with Annie, and she didn't know that Annie's mom didn't even want her to be my friend. Maybe Annie's dad didn't want her to be friends with me either. After all, she hadn't talked to me since before Thanksgiving. I could just imagine what would happen if Mom called Carson Rothschild. He would refuse to write a letter for her, and then he would tell Annie all about it. Annie and her dad don't talk that much; still, I didn't want to take the risk. It would be even more humiliating.

"You only know Mr. Rothschild because I'm friends with Annie," I told Mom. "You put me in the sentencing memo, and now you want to call my friend's father. I feel like you're using me."

"If that's the way you feel, then I won't do it," Mom said.

I knew I had hurt her feelings. Even though I was mad at her, I didn't want to do that. But I nodded.

"Okay," Mom said.

"I'm really tired," I told her. "I'm going to take a nap now."

"All right," Mom said. "I'll get out of your way and turn off the lights."

"No, it's okay," I said. "I'm going to go up to my room."

I stood up from the couch, the afghan still wrapped around me. I felt a little dizzy, and not just because my head was all stuffed up. I made my way across the room toward the stairs. I could feel Mom watching me as I walked away.

chapter eighteen

I went back to school the next day. Annie was basically pretending that I didn't even exist anymore. I have two classes with her—American Government & Law and Pre-Algebra. We have assigned seats in American Government, because Mrs. Harrity doesn't believe in letting students pick where they want to sit, so Annie and I sit across the room from each other. In Pre-Algebra we always used to sit next to each other, but she had switched seats the day she had confronted me about lunch with Alex Jedder.

Jordan and I weren't really friends anymore, either. She didn't ignore me the way Annie did. She still was nice to me if she saw me in the hall, but she ate lunch with Annie every day, which meant she didn't eat with me. Lauren tried her best to be fair about the whole thing. She took turns eating with me and Annie. On the days Lauren went to lunch with Annie and Jordan, it was really hard. I ate with Elana Bronstein, or Ellie Oxberg, or Lily O'Mara, but there were times I felt like they didn't want to be with me either. Maybe it was because of Mom, but also I think they just didn't want to make Annie angry. Annie is the kind of popular that's almost dangerous. She seemed powerful; nobody wants to be on her bad side. Even people who don't like her still don't want to cross her.

I started thinking about what makes people popular. You have to be sort of tough. You can't always be yourself. Like Ginny Winkler, for example: She would do better if she didn't talk to herself and say whatever popped into her head. I was less popular now that people knew the truth about my mom.

It could all be taken away so quickly. I used to take it for granted—I was safe because I was Annie's best friend. She picked me over everyone else, when the truth is she could've been best friends with anyone. It used to make me feel lucky. Now I felt so stupid, even though nothing about me had changed. I wasn't the one who had broken the law. I wondered what would happen to Annie if everyone found out that her mom got drunk all the time. To be honest I wished there were a way for people to find out about Mrs. Rothschild without me actually being the one to tell them. Then Annie would see that being popular didn't mean anything; it didn't mean you were a good person, or better than anyone else.

And yet I still wanted to be popular.

"Hey, Carly, welcome back," Alex said when I walked into the science room for third period. "I missed you."

"Yeah, right," I said.

"No, really," he said, smiling his Alex smile. "I missed you like crazy. I was bleeding inside."

"Well, I'm back now," I said, "so you can stop bleeding."

Alex had his books piled on the table. When he flipped open his notebook, an envelope slipped out, red with black swirly writing. It looked like an invitation to something important, and I knew it had to be Annie's birthday invitation. It was just like the Rothschilds to hire someone to address the envelopes in calligraphy.

Alex picked it up and jammed it in between the pages of his textbook. I wondered what Annie would think if she saw him wrinkling her precious invite. "I guess everyone's going to Annie's party, huh?" Alex asked.

I shrugged. I didn't want to tell him I hadn't been invited. Alex hadn't ever made a big deal about things with Mom. Sometimes I wondered if he even knew about it. I mean, he had to know, but that was the thing about boys—they just didn't seem to care about the same things girls did. They didn't gossip as much.

Just then Dr. Sherman clapped his hands. "Attention, ladies and gentlemen," he said.

"Here he goes again," Alex muttered, but I was just happy to change the subject.

I had American Government for fourth period, which meant I was in class with Annie. Mrs. Harrity showed us a video, which was a nice break from actually having to pay attention. It was something about a guy named Gideon who was poor and didn't have money for a lawyer, and his case ended up in the Supreme Court. But it was really hard to pay attention to the movie with Annie right there across the table from me. I thought about the last time we had stopped speaking, which was back in fifth grade. She had been bragging about how she was so good at gymnastics that she would definitely get to be on the cheerleading squad in high school. It was getting annoying, because I couldn't even touch my toes, and there was no way I'd get to be on the squad with her. Later that day I told Elana Bronstein that I thought Maggie Newell was actually the best gymnast in our grade. She could jump up and do splits in the air, which was something that even Annie couldn't do.

I was right, and Elana totally agreed with me, but I have to admit that it wasn't a nice thing to say about my best friend. Annie somehow found out about it, and she was really mad. (If you want to know the truth, I think Elana told Jordan, because she and Jordan were best friends back then, and then Jordan spread it around, because she loves gossiping.) Anyway, Annie wouldn't talk to me. She sent Jordan over to tell me that I was mean and jealous. I told Jordan to tell Annie that she was a stuck-up snob.

Jordan shuttled between the two of us for the rest of the day, but by the next morning it was boring to talk through her. Annie came up to me and said if I was really her best friend I would tell people that she was the best gymnast no matter what. I told her that I was sorry and I didn't mean to hurt her feelings. And we made up. Things get more complicated when you get older, but I wished it could be like that again.

The video ended, and Mrs. Harrity turned the lights on. The room was suddenly bright again, and it made my eyes hurt. "We've only got about three minutes left of the period, so we can end for today," Mrs. Harrity said. It was so unlike her to let us out early. Usually she makes us stay until the exact second that the bell rings, but maybe she had to go to the bathroom or something. Or maybe, just maybe, she was trying to be nice. After all, she had just let us watch a video for the whole period. "And just in case any of you tried to daydream your way through class today," Mrs. Harrity added, "there will be a quiz on *Gideon versus Wainwright* tomorrow."

Of course getting to watch a movie in class was too good to be true when it came to Mrs. Harrity. I had been thinking about Annie the whole time. I would have to look up *Gideon v. Wainwright* on the Internet when I got home. I hoped there would be information about it. Annie's seat was closer to the door. I watched her stand up and gather her textbook, notebook, and pen. I wondered what she and Jordan were going to do for lunch.

It was my day to eat with Lauren, and we were going to Slice of Life. I went to my locker and unloaded my books from my backpack, and then I headed down the hall to wait for her. After a couple minutes the other classes started letting out, and the hallway filled up. Lauren bounded over to me, grinning. "Guess what—I got an A on the last algebra quiz," she said.

"Congratulations," I said.

"I'm so relieved. My parents were seriously flipping out."

It was so weird that Lauren's parents would flip out over anything, since they basically have a perfect daughter. "I knew you could do it," I told her.

"Thanks," she said. She turned the dial on her locker, and it popped open. The inside of Lauren's locker looks exactly the way you would expect it to: neat and orderly. The books are lined up in size order, and all her binders have labels on the edges so she knows which goes with what subject. Lauren says she keeps everything neat so she never has to do a major cleanup. At the beginning of each year I always mean to keep my locker neat, but somehow it doesn't end up that way. By the time school lets out in June, my locker is a disaster.

Lauren bent down and started rustling through her backpack. I watched her pull out a binder, a folder, and her math textbook. The binder and folder were both green, which matched the green of the textbook. I looked for a flash of red paper with black swirly letters, but I didn't see any. Maybe Lauren had the invitation at home, or maybe she had it tucked into a folder so I wouldn't see it. "I heard Annie sent out her invitations," I said.

"Did Jordan tell you?" Lauren asked.

"No," I said. "I didn't actually hear it from anyone. I saw a red envelope in Alex Jedder's notebook, and I figured out what it was."

"She just sent them out a couple days ago," Lauren said. "I should've warned you, but I didn't want to make you feel bad."

"Is she having a movie-star theme with a red carpet?" I asked.

"I think so," Lauren said slowly.

"That was my idea," I told her.

"You're not angry at me, are you?" Lauren asked.

"No, of course not," I said. "I knew you were going to be invited, and I knew I wasn't going to be."

"I told her what really happened at lunch that day—you know, that you weren't really trying to have a secret lunch with Alex Jedder."

"What did she say?"

Lauren sighed. "It doesn't really matter," she said. I knew that meant that Annie had said something awful about Mom. "People in glass houses shouldn't throw stones."

"I don't know what that means," I told her.

"Everyone's parents can be weird sometimes," Lauren said. "I don't judge you for it, and I don't think Annie should either. It's just, I'm friends with you both, and that's hard sometimes."

"You don't have to be friends with me if you don't want to," I said defensively.

"Of course I want to," she insisted. "I didn't mean it like that."

"I'm sorry," I said.

"Forget about Annie," Lauren said. "She's being completely immature."

I wanted to ask Lauren why she was still friends with Annie if she thought Annie was so immature, even though none of what was happening was Lauren's fault.

How did Lauren stay popular anyway? I wondered what her secret was, but it wasn't the kind of thing I could ask her about. She was like the exception to the popularity rule: She was never fake, and she didn't always give in to Annie. She stayed friends with me; in fact she was probably the reason why Elana, Ellie, and Lily were still mostly nice to me. I knew I owed her a lot.

"Come on, we better get going or we'll never get a table," Lauren said.

We headed over to Slice of Life. The booths were all taken up, but there were two seats next to each other at the counter, and we sat there and ordered our slices and sodas. The pizza came out piping hot. I could see the oil glistening on the top, and I grabbed a few napkins to soak it up. I couldn't get Annie's party out of my head. The thing was, I still thought of Annie as my best friend. She probably called Jordan her best friend now, but I couldn't replace Annie that easily—not even with Lauren. I liked her a lot, but it wasn't the same.

This eighth grader Kelly Ryder came up to the counter and grabbed a couple of napkins. She walked away, and Lauren leaned toward me. "I know it's awful, but I can't look at her without remembering what happened to her and Carter at the Renaissance Fair last year," she said.

"I know," I said. Carter Liss is Kelly's boyfriend. They've been dating since they were in sixth grade, and they've been together longer than any other couple at Preston. They're like the poster couple of the school. Last year at the Renaissance Fair they were kissing, and their braces got stuck together. Lauren and I didn't see it, but Jordan did. She told us they stayed stuck together until one of the teachers came and pulled them apart. Carter is really tall, like Faux Pa, so I could just imagine him hunched over, attached to Kelly's face. Jordan said it was the most embarrassing thing she'd ever seen.

"They'll probably get married one day and tell the story to their kids," Lauren said.

It must be cool to already know who you want to marry when you're only in middle school. Once, Annie and I made predictions for our lives—like when our weddings would be and how many kids we would have, boys or girls, and what their names would be. I wanted two girls. Annie wanted a boy, then a girl. We knew for sure that we wanted to live in big houses right next door to each other. I would have a tennis court in my backyard, and she would have a pool in hers, and we could share them both. Our kids would be best friends too.

We wrote it all down, then sealed it up in an envelope and put it at the back of her desk drawer. Across the front she had written: *Do not open for ten years.* The stupidest thing was that we hadn't written the date, so we wouldn't be able to remember ten years from when. But now it didn't matter, because we wouldn't get those houses next door to each other, and our kids wouldn't be best friends. I guess it was silly to think we could predict the future, but it made me really sad.

At the end of the day I took the bus home. It stops a couple of blocks away from our house. Two other kids get off at the same place I do, but they turn right to go home, and I turn left, so I always walk those last blocks on my own.

I noticed that people had started to put up their Christmas lights. It wasn't dark out yet, so they weren't turned on, but I could see that they were there. Mom thinks the multicolored lights are kind of tacky. She lets us have the white ones, but when I was little I always wanted to have more colors and string them up all over the house. Faux Pa would take Jessa, Justin, and me for a drive all around Westchester so we could see the lights on all the houses. Some people really went all out. Their front lawns looked like winter wonderlands, with fake snow, reindeer, and about a million lights. Faux Pa said their electric bills must be astronomical.

It was cold out, but I was walking slowly, just thinking about Christmas lights and how people would be celebrating the holidays this year like it was any other year. Then I heard footsteps. I turned to glance behind me, and I saw a man—at least I was pretty sure it was a man. He was wearing a hooded sweatshirt, and I couldn't see his face. I guess it could've been a woman. I turned back around and started walking faster.

My heart was pumping hard. In sixth grade this woman came to speak to our school. Her name was Peggy Anson, and she taught self-defense. The Preston administration brought her in because someone had been attacked in a town not too far away. We were pulled out of class so we could learn how to kick someone so it really hurt, and how to poke someone in the eye without getting your finger stuck. We all thought it was so gross that you could actually get your finger stuck in someone else's eyeball. But Peggy Anson was really serious about it. She said we should hold our pointer and middle fingers together and poke someone with both fingers. She also said we should carry our keys in our hands and never wear ponytails so no one could grab us from behind.

I could still hear the footsteps behind me. What if it was a criminal? What would a criminal be doing wandering the streets of New Rochelle? Maybe he had just escaped from prison. My hair was up in a ponytail, and my keys were in my backpack. I could just imagine him grabbing me.

I started to run, sweating despite the cold. I was afraid to turn around again in case he was following. By the time I got to my house, there was no sign of him. I dropped my backpack on the stoop and opened up the little pocket in the front to get my key, and then the craziest thing occurred to me: Mom was a criminal too.

chapter nineteen

Amelia came over the night of Annie's party. It was the first time I'd invited anyone to my house since the day Mom was arrested. The doorbell rang and made the same *ring RING ring* sound it makes at Amelia's house, only a little lower. "Who is it?" I had learned my lesson.

"It's me, Amelia."

When I opened the door, Amelia and her mom were standing on the front stoop. I wondered why Mrs. Sarsen was there. Amelia and I were way too old to need our mothers to walk us across the street. Maybe Mrs. Sarsen felt like she had to protect Amelia from my mom now.

"Hey," Amelia said. She was carrying her overnight bag. Mrs. Sarsen was holding a pie, which I was sure she had baked herself. She isn't the kind of person who ever brings over ready-made pies.

If she wanted to protect Amelia from Mom, would

she have let Amelia pack an overnight bag? Would she have baked for us?

"Hi," I said.

"Hi, honey," Mrs. Sarsen said. "How are you?"

"Good," I said.

"I'm glad to hear it," Mrs. Sarsen said. She smiled, and her eyes got squinty the way Amelia's did when she smiled. I'd never realized that they smiled in the exact same way. Their lips spread really thin, and their teeth are perfectly white and straight. Amelia will never need braces.

They were still standing on the stoop. The whole thing was getting awkward. "Do you want to come in?"

"Thanks," Mrs. Sarsen said. She stepped inside, and Amelia followed. "Are your parents home?"

"My mom is," I said. "Faux Pa went to his office to do some work." The end of the semester was coming up, and Faux Pa was writing the final exams for his students. He always works longer hours at the end of the semester, but part of me still wondered if he went to work to avoid being home with Mom.

"I love that you call him Faux Pa," Mrs. Sarsen said. She was smiling kindly, but I still felt suspicious. "What about Jessa and Justin?"

"They're with Jocelyn this weekend," I said.

"Right," Mrs. Sarsen said. "Well, can you tell your mom that I'm here?"

I nodded. I was having flashbacks to when the FBI came to the door and asked me the same thing, even though I knew Mrs. Sarsen wasn't about to handcuff her or anything like that. "I'll go get her," I said.

I ran upstairs to Mom's room. She was sitting on the

bed, flipping through papers. "I thought I heard the doorbell," she said.

"Yeah," I said. "Amelia just got here. And Mrs. Sarsen's here, too. She wants to talk to you."

Mom put her hand to her forehead like she suddenly had a headache, but she came back downstairs with me. Amelia and her mom were in the foyer. Amelia hadn't even taken her jacket off. I was trying to figure out what everything meant. Mrs. Sarsen held the pie out toward Mom. "This is for you."

"Thanks, Susan," Mom said, taking it from her.

"Well, you know me. I can't walk into anyone's house without bringing baked goods. This is one of my latest creations."

"I'm sure we'll enjoy it," Mom said. She sounded strange, almost formal. She put the pie down on the table next to the stairwell. "Is this all right for Amelia to eat?"

"No, but she has a few gluten-free cookies in her bag, so she's all set."

"Good to know," Mom said.

"I wanted to come sooner," Mrs. Sarsen said. "I sent a card along with the cookies Amelia and Carly made, but I didn't hear back from you, so . . ." Her voice trailed off.

I looked over at Mom. She had given me the cookies from Amelia, but she hadn't said anything about a card from Mrs. Sarsen. Now her eyes were shiny. "I got it," Mom said. "It meant a lot."

"I've been thinking of you," Mrs. Sarsen continued. "I've been hoping to bump into you. I didn't want to bother you, but I look for you every time I leave the house. I hope you don't mind that I came today. When

Carly invited Amelia over, I thought it was a good excuse to drop by."

"It's okay," Mom said.

"I don't know the rules for this, Leigh," Mrs. Sarsen said. "I've never had a friend go through this before."

Mrs. Sarsen put her hand on Mom's shoulder, but Mom shook her head. "I couldn't face you before," Mom said. "I couldn't lie and say I didn't do it. And now with the guilty plea, I'm just so ashamed. It's hard to even look at you. You always came to my rescue. You always believed in me. Now look at the mess I'm in."

"I'm not perfect either, Leigh," Mrs. Sarsen said.

"You've never made a mistake like this," Mom told her.

"Maybe not."

"Everyone's so disappointed in me. They're so angry."

"You're still my friend," Mrs. Sarsen said.

The four of us were quiet. I felt frozen where I was standing, like time had stopped and we were waiting for someone to press a button and make it start again. Finally, Mom said, "I could use a friend right about now."

Mrs. Sarsen wrapped her arms around Mom. I could tell Mom had started to cry. They held on to each other for a while—longer than hugs usually last. Amelia and I just looked at each other. I felt so guilty, because Mrs. Sarsen was being much nicer to Mom than I had been. Finally, Mom pulled away.

"Girls, give us a few minutes, will you?" Mrs. Sarsen asked.

Amelia pulled on my arm. "Okay," I said.

We went into the den. Amelia finally took her jacket off. We were both being kind of quiet because of what had just happened. It's hard to know what to say after you see something like that. We sat on the couch. I turned on the TV and flipped through the channels. "Is there anything you want to watch?"

"I want to watch whatever you want to watch," Amelia said. See what I mean how she was the sidekick? Not like Annie, who always had an opinion about what we should watch.

There wasn't anything on that I really wanted to see, so I just stopped on one of those celebrity news shows. They were talking about a movie premiere in Hollywood, which made me think about Annie's party. The party that was *my* idea. Wouldn't you think she would've changed the theme since she was so mad at me?

Part of the reason I had invited Amelia over was so I wouldn't have to think about Annie, but I couldn't help myself. I was sure the Rothschilds had gone all out to make it look like a real red-carpet party. They probably had fake paparazzi lined up, taking pictures of everyone as they arrived. If Annie and I were still friends and I had gone, I would've worn my blue dress. Mom had gotten it for me over the summer. There were feathers stitched together to make straps, and there were little feathers, like fringe, along the bottom. Mom said the dress was like a work of art. It was just like Mom to compare a dress to something that should be in a museum.

I wondered what Annie had ended up wearing. When we'd first talked about the party, she had said she wanted Mom to hook her up with something from the *Lovelock Falls* wardrobe. Obviously that hadn't happened, but I was sure Mrs. Rothschild had bought Annie something fabulous.

"And now," the TV announcer said, "the secret to beautiful, clear skin. Dermatologist to the stars Dr. Elizabeth Crawford created a vitamin-enriched serum for her celebrity clients. It's expensive, but worth it."

"You're so lucky you have such great skin," Amelia said.

"So do you," I said.

She shook her head. "I got my first pimple."

"I don't see anything," I said.

She pointed to the faintest little red mark on her chin. "Here," she said.

"That's not even a pimple. It's just a dot."

"It's mostly gone now, but you should've seen it a few days ago. I was really stressed out from this social studies project we had to do, and stress gives you pimples. There's this girl in my class who's always stressed out about school and her face is totally broken out. I feel so bad for her."

"I'm surprised I don't have tons of pimples then," I said. "It's been really stressful over here."

"Well, stress isn't the only thing," Amelia said. "My mom says I shouldn't eat food that's too greasy. It's really annoying, because it's hard enough for me to eat already."

"I always wipe the grease off my pizza," I said. "Maybe that's helping me not get pimples."

"How come the people on TV never seem to break out?" Amelia asked.

"They do," I said. "They just wear a lot of makeup so you can't tell."

I knew that from sitting in the makeup room at *Lovelock Falls*. Once when I was visiting the set, I saw this actress Delia Fields have a complete meltdown because she had a pimple on the side of her nose. She'd squeezed it to try and get rid of it, but it just looked red and irritated and even bigger than before. "It's like a volcano erupted on my face," she cried. "I've always wondered what it would be like to be ugly, and now I am. This could ruin my whole career." She threw a brush across the room. It banged against the wall and left a little black mark on the white paint, but no one got mad at her. She buried her face in her hands. The makeup artist came over and promised to cover it up. She kept telling Delia not to cry, because the tears would streak her makeup.

I know it sounds ridiculous, like I'm exaggerating the story, but really, that's what happened. Afterward, Mom told me that Delia Fields was the most melodramatic person she'd ever met.

I didn't tell Amelia about it. I knew if everything with Mom hadn't happened, I would've told her. But it felt strange to talk about *Lovelock Falls* now.

There was another segment about a child star who was all grown up and designing handbags. The reporter was exclaiming over the different styles, even though they were really ugly. Then the show ended, and the news came on. I started flipping channels again.

"Hey, you two," Amelia's mother said. I turned away from the TV. Mrs. Sarsen was standing in the doorway. "Come on; we're going to have a girls' night out."

"I thought you were having dinner with Dad and Billy," Amelia said.

Mrs. Sarsen shook her head. "I called Dad and told him he and Billy should have a boys' night. Leigh said Jonathan will probably be working late, but we'll leave him a note and he can join them if he wants."

"Where are we going?"

"There's a place by the water in Poughkeepsie with a full gluten-free menu. It's a bit of a drive, so we should get going."

I knew we were going to Poughkeepsie because it was far away enough that no one would know Mom. Amelia and I went to the foyer and put our jackets on.

Dinner ended up being a lot of fun. The food was really good, even if it was gluten-free. Mom and Mrs. Sarsen started talking about all the things they used to do with Amelia and me when we were young—like taking us to the Wiggles concert, the first time we went on a merry-go-round, and how Amelia used to always get diarrhea after she ate, before they realized she had celiac disease.

"That's gross," Amelia said.

"And that gymnastics class," Mom said. "The one in Mamaroneck with the instructor who dressed like a kid stuck in the eighties—she wore those leotards with puff paint all over them."

"Right," Mrs. Sarsen said. "Gina's Gym. I don't think it even exists anymore."

"My mother had bought Carly the lessons for her birthday, and Carly was all excited about it."

"I don't remember ever doing gymnastics," I said. "I can't even touch my toes."

"You were a toddler," Mom said. "You loved it. You used to pretend everything was a balance beam. You'd walk along the edge of the sidewalk and hold out your arms to steady yourself. It was very cute."

"And of course Amelia wanted to go because you were going, so I signed her up too," Mrs. Sarsen said.

"We had a great routine. Leigh and I would drop you off on Saturday mornings, go out for brunch, and then pick you up."

"And then came the talent show Gina put on for the parents," Mom said. "She had you all lined up, and she called on each kid, one by one, to demonstrate a different activity—bars, cartwheels, somersaults. Finally, it was time for the balance beam. Gina called out some kid's name."

"That girl Annika, with the white-blond hair," Mrs. Sarsen said.

"Right," Mom said. "But my little Carly popped up instead. You jumped right up on that beam, your arms outstretched. You had practiced so much. But Gina was yelling at you to come down because it wasn't your turn. You were so upset about it that you fell off and cried and cried."

"I can still picture this in my head like it was yesterday," Mrs. Sarsen said. "Amelia started crying too, just because Carly was crying."

"I don't remember that," Amelia said.

"Me either," I said, my cheeks flushing. "That doesn't sound like me at all."

"It wasn't really like you," Mom said. "But I think you just loved the beam so much, and you wanted to show me what you were capable of. It's so funny to remember—at the time I was so embarrassed. No one else's kid was carrying on like that."

I wondered if that was Lauren's secret—not the crying part, but being the kind of kid who would just jump up on the beam, bold and unafraid. I wished I could still be that way. Mom grinned and reached over to squeeze my hand. I smiled back. Right then she seemed so much like my old mom, and it felt like none of the other stuff even existed—*Lovelock Falls*, Mom's guilty plea, her upcoming sentencing, and Annie having a birthday party without me.

Suddenly, the waiter came over to our table with a huge piece of cake. He placed it in front of Mom and started singing the happy-birthday song. The candle was flickering. Mom's birthday wasn't for months. She looked about as confused as I felt. "What?" she asked.

"Go with it, Leigh," Mrs. Sarsen said. She sang along with the waiter. When the song ended, Mrs. Sarsen told Mom to make a wish. She closed her eyes and blew out the flame. I was sure I knew what she was wishing for.

"Enjoy," the waiter said, dropping four forks on the table. "It's on the house."

He walked away. "You told them it was my birthday?" Mom asked. Mrs. Sarsen nodded. "Why? We don't need the cake—we have a pie you made waiting for us at home."

"But I know you're going to miss celebrating your birthday this coming year," Mrs. Sarsen said. "I wanted you to have some birthday cake."

Mom's eyes were shiny again, but she blinked quickly and smiled. "I thought I would just get to skip my birthday this year and stay young," she said.

"Oh, no," Mrs. Sarsen said. "If I have to get older, then you do too."

"Fair enough," Mom said. "But this is way too big a piece for me to eat on my own. Come on, everyone, dig in."

chapter twenty

Christmas at our house wasn't very merry at all. Jessa and Justin were in Florida with Jocelyn, visiting Jocelyn's sister Marilyn. Mom, Faux Pa, and I didn't go away, because Mom wasn't really allowed to go anywhere, and Faux Pa said we had to save money. He and Mom didn't even buy as many presents as usual. They didn't get anything for each other. Mom gave me a silver bracelet with my initials engraved on top. It was very pretty, but I knew I would always think of it as the present I got right before she was sent away.

Basically, that was all we thought about. We were just sitting around the house, waiting for Mom's sentencing. The sentencing memo had been finished and filed with the court. Mom would be appearing before Judge Thompson the first week of January, right before the end of winter vacation.

Waiting has always been one of my least favorite

things to do. It just seems like a waste of time, like empty space. I like to get to the next thing. Faux Pa always says that's the problem with my generation—we are used to instant gratification, so we don't even know how to wait. We get e-mail instead of waiting for mail to be delivered; we can call people on cell phones instead of having to wait for the person to get home and call us back; we can even fast-forward through commercials when we watch things on the DVR. One night last year we went out for a family dinner, and the food was taking a really long time. The people at the table across from us had sat down at least twenty minutes after us, but their food came first. Justin started moaning about it, and then Jessa and I joined in. Faux Pa gave us a whole lecture about how we needed to learn to be patient. "Patience is a virtue," he said.

"There's nothing virtuous about waiting an hour for your food in a restaurant that is clearly subpar," Jessa said.

"What does that mean?" Justin asked.

"It means this place sucks," Jessa told him.

Mom has always said that Jessa is brutally honest. Faux Pa says that sometimes she's just brutal.

Anyway, I think Faux Pa is big on patience because he's a scientist. He's used to having to wait for experiments to work, for theories to be proven. When he works at home, he spreads all his stuff out on the dining-room table. Sometimes when I walk past him, he's not reading or writing anything, just staring off into space, like he knows that if he just waits long enough, the answers will come to him.

But I didn't mind waiting for Mom's sentencing. In

fact I hoped something would happen so we'd have to keep waiting. There could be a big fire at the courthouse, or maybe Judge Thompson would be in an accident and have to spend a long time recuperating. I know it's not the nicest thing to imagine disasters happening to other people, but I couldn't help myself. If her sentencing went on as planned, she would be gone before winter break was even over.

I just hoped Judge Thompson would think Mom was a good person. I hoped he would think the good stuff in the sentencing memo mattered more than the bad stuff Mom and Vivette had done.

The day after Christmas, Mom started cleaning—not just dusting and putting stuff away, but going through drawers and file cabinets, getting rid of things she didn't need. I walked into her room. The TV was on, even though Mom wasn't really watching it. She was in front of her closet, her back to me, flipping through her clothes and occasionally tossing a shirt or a scarf behind her. There were piles of clothes on the floor and on the bed. Sometimes I thought about how Mrs. Sarsen had stepped forward in the foyer and hugged Mom the way she had. There was a part of me that wanted to throw my arms around Mom too, but it felt like something was holding me back.

"Hey, Mom," I said.

She turned around, her face flushed. Her hair was in a ponytail, and I could see little tendrils escaping around the edges, thinner and lighter than the rest of her hair. The way the light hit them, they looked lit up, sort of translucent, like a spiderweb. Mom rubbed her forehead with the back of her hand. The lines on her face made her seem so old, and that scared me. "Hi, honey," she said. "What are you up to?"

"Nothing, really," I said.

"I'm sorry," she said. "I know this isn't the Christmas break you had in mind." I shrugged. I didn't know what I'd had in mind. I just knew it wasn't this. "Are all your friends away?"

"Pretty much," I said.

When you go to a private school, kids generally go away during the school breaks. Annie goes on spectacular vacations. Every winter her parents rent a villa somewhere tropical. I knew from Lauren that this year they were in Bermuda, in a house with actual servants. They just had to step outside and they were on a private beach.

"Well, I have a project for you," Mom said. "Why don't you go through everything here and see if there's anything you want to keep?" She gestured to the clothes lying around her.

"You're giving your clothes away?"

"There's a lot I don't need," she said. "I'm going to be gone for a while."

"I know you pled guilty so the prosecutor will tell the judge you should go away for a year."

"That's right," Mom said.

"But Dale said the judge makes the final decision about that. So isn't it possible that he'll decide that you don't need to be sent away at all?"

"I guess anything is possible," Mom said. "But honey, that's not going to happen. I'm just hoping he won't send me away for longer."

"You're coming back," I reminded her. "No matter what, you're coming back."

"Of course I am," she said. "But Dale says the food in prison isn't too great, and I'm planning to get really skinny on the Great Prison Diet."

She was trying to lighten the mood, but I didn't feel like smiling. "You're already skinny," I said.

"I know, hon," Mom said. "The truth is, I have more than I'll ever use."

She's simplifying her life before she goes away, I thought. But I knew it wasn't what Ally's guru had had in mind.

"Anyway," Mom continued, "I promised Faux Pa I would clean everything out. He thinks maybe we can sell some of it online. You know he's worried about money."

"Yeah, I know," I said. "But do you think people would buy these clothes if they know they were yours? I mean . . ." I wasn't sure how to say what I meant; I meant would people want to buy things from a criminal.

"I don't know," Mom said. "We can do it anonymously. But if there's anything you want, we'll set it aside." She reached down and picked up a skirt that had been lying on the floor. "Like this," she said, holding it up by the hanger. It was a black skirt, on the short side, but not too short. The fabric was layered and wrinkly, but in a way that you knew it was supposed to be wrinkled. There were brown and cream flowers stitched up the side. Mom shook the hanger so the skirt swayed a little, like in a breeze. It was beautiful.

"I don't want it," I said. "It would feel weird to wear it."

"Yes, maybe this is a little too mature for you," Mom said. That wasn't what I had meant, and I had a feeling she knew. She held the skirt out and just stared at it for a couple seconds, like she was saying good-bye.

Then she put it back on top of the pile on the floor.

I didn't want to go through the rest of Mom's closet with her, but I didn't want to leave her either. I walked back to the bed and rearranged the clothes on it so there was space for me to sit down and watch TV.

Watching TV is the perfect activity when you don't know what else to do, when you don't even really want to think. Mom kept cleaning, and I picked up the remote and flipped through the channels until I found something I wanted to watch—a Brody Hudson movie Annie and I had seen last summer. I turned up the volume a little bit. I could still hear Mom clanging hangers, occasionally mumbling to herself. There was something really comforting about having her there. We were each doing our own thing, but I liked knowing she was there, near me, in case I needed her. That's where a mother should be.

chapter twenty-one

Mom's sentencing was on a Monday, a couple days after New Year's. School would be starting up again in two days, on Wednesday. We never go back to school on the Monday after a long vacation—another private-school thing. It's like the administration wants to stretch the break as long as possible.

It was hard to even think about going back to school. All that mattered was that today was Monday. I picked out a black skirt and charcoal-gray sweater to wear. I once heard Mom say it was important to have a black suit in your closet in case you needed something to wear to a funeral. That's what I thought about when I got dressed. I didn't have a black suit, so I wore the closest thing I could find. I put on black tights—not stockings—and my pointy-toe loafers with a little heel.

The sentencing was set for one o'clock, but we went to the lawyers' office first. Dale Addie and Jamie

Berkell met us in the reception area and led us into the same conference room we'd been in the last time. Debbie brought in bottles of water. There were bagels on a tray in the center of the table. Jamie said we should help ourselves because it would be a long day, but my heart was pounding, and I felt like if I put anything in my mouth, even just a sip of water, I would probably throw up. Mom was in the seat next to me, and Faux Pa was on my other side. I wasn't looking at him; I was looking at Mom. She was sitting up very straight. I kept thinking about how it was actually going to happen today. We had been waiting and waiting, and now, in a few short hours, it would all be over. Faux Pa and I would be driving home, and Mom would probably be on her way to prison.

Dale Addie went over what we should expect when we got to the courthouse. She said there might be a couple of reporters because of the *Lovelock Falls* connection. "I anticipate the hearing itself will be very straightforward," Dale said. "There will be a court reporter taking everything down for the record. You took a plea and accepted responsibility. The prosecution is asking for the lower end of the sentencing guidelines. As I told you, I think Judge Thompson will agree to that."

Mom nodded. "Okay," she said.

"If that's what happens, then after the hearing you'll be in the custody of the Bureau of Prisons," Dale continued. "A court marshal will handcuff you and escort you from the courtroom. They'll process you locally, and then you will be taken to the prison, the facility in Pennsylvania that we talked about."

Mom had told me about the prison in Pennsylvania—about three hours away from where we lived, the kind of prison called a camp, which meant it was minimum security, for people who were convicted of white-collar crimes. It wasn't like those horrible prisons you see in the movies, the kind with the thick cement walls and barbed wire to keep murderers from escaping. But it wasn't like Mom would be at a spa, either. She'd share a room with a bunch of other white-collar prisoners, and she wouldn't be able to leave.

"Do you have anything to add?" Dale asked Jamie.

"The jewelry," Jamie said.

"Right," Dale said. She turned to Mom. "We need to act under the assumption that you're going to be taken into custody after the hearing, so you shouldn't be wearing anything of value—no jewelry. Whatever you have, give it to Jonathan to take home."

"I'm not wearing anything valuable," Mom said. She held up her left hand, and it shook a little. "I'm not even wearing my wedding band."

Mom and Faux Pa have matching wedding bands. I used to hold Mom's hand and spin the ring around her finger. On the inside, the part you can't see, Faux Pa's initials are engraved. Mom's initials are engraved on the inside of Faux Pa's ring. Faux Pa hadn't seemed so mad at her lately. Now he acted like she was someone he didn't know very well; they just happened to live in the same house. And after today they might not even live in the same house. I wondered if he would take his wedding band off too, once Mom was gone.

"All right," Dale said. "Do you have any friends coming today?"

"Yes," Mom said. "My friend Susan, and Jonathan's friend Eric and his wife."

I had been surprised when Mom told me people were coming to the sentencing, but she said Dale had told her to invite them. "That's good," Dale said. "It's nice for the judge to see you have people supporting you. Do you want to practice your statement again?"

"No," Mom said.

"Any questions for me?"

"No," Mom said again.

"All right," Dale said. "Jamie and I are going to step out for a few minutes so you three can have some time. We'll come back in when it's time to go. I suggest that you ride with us, Leigh, in case there's a scene over at the courthouse. Jonathan and Carly can follow."

"Okay," Mom said. Dale and Jamie walked out of the room. We were all just quiet. I didn't know what to say. I knew there probably were things I should tell Mom—things you should say when you know you might not see someone for a long time. Faux Pa and I would visit her in prison, but it wouldn't be the same. I watched Mom stand up and walk the length of the room. She was wearing her black pencil skirt and a blazer. She looked so good, like herself, the way I always remembered her looking. It was impossible for Mom to not look fashionable.

Jamie came back in after a few minutes. I noticed that his hair looked extra gelled. He was wearing a camel-colored coat. The wool looked really soft, the kind of fabric you want to reach out and touch. "Are you ready to get going?" he asked.

It wasn't like we would really ever feel ready to go to Mom's sentencing, but we stood up and put our coats on. Dale was already in the reception area, and she walked us out to the parking lot. I followed Faux Pa to his gray sedan. When he first got it a couple years ago, Justin named it Viper. I never thought the name fit right. To me it looked more like a Fred or a Marty. Sometimes Justin would talk about the car like it was a person: *Can we take Viper to get ice cream? Put the pedal to the metal so Viper goes super fast.* Not that Faux Pa ever drives super fast, but Justin always wanted him to.

Faux Pa unlocked the doors, and I got into the passenger side of the car. He waited for me to put on my seat belt, and then he put the key in the ignition. I listened to the sound of the engine turning over. It had started to drizzle a little bit—not enough to need an umbrella, but enough so Faux Pa had to flip on the windshield wipers and clear off the speckles of water.

"We've had a lot of rain this season," Faux Pa said.

I nodded in agreement, even though I knew he was looking at the road and not at me. The wipers rubbed hard against the window. I didn't really care about the rain. I looked out the window at the passing cars. There were so many people. It's funny to pass by people in cars and then never ever see them again. The world felt big. I wondered where everyone else was headed. I bet they would never guess that I was on my way to court, to my mother's sentencing. They would have no idea that today was one of the worst, most important days of my life. It was like there was something caught in my chest, or like someone was squeezing it. I felt tight and uncomfortable. Behind us a siren whooped, and Faux Pa switched lanes so an ambulance could pass.

A few minutes later Faux Pa parked Viper in a lot, and then we crossed the street to the courthouse. He took my hand as we walked up the concrete steps. My hands were cold but also sweaty. I was embarrassed that he had to hold my sweaty hand, but I didn't let go. Mom was already in the lobby with Dale and Jamie. "We got lucky," Dale said. "I didn't see any cameras." I thought to myself: *Lucky would be if this hadn't happened. Lucky would be if the courthouse suddenly caught fire, the records were all destroyed, and we got to go home.*

Judge Thompson's courtroom was on the third floor. We took the elevator and went down a hallway. Jamie opened the door to peek inside. "It looks like we're the first ones here," he said.

"Let's go in and get settled," Dale said.

Jamie held the door open for all of us. I saw Judge Thompson's "bench" at the far end of the room. Two tables were in front of it—the table for Dale, Jamie, and Mom, and then the table for the prosecution. And then, behind the tables, there were several rows of seats for people who wanted to watch. Jamie walked up to one of the tables, the one on the left side of the room, and put down his briefcase. I watched him pull out a couple of manila folders, a pad of paper, and pens. Faux Pa took off his coat, folded it up, and placed it on one of the seats behind the table. "Do you want to give me your jacket, Carly?" he asked.

I shook my head. "No, thanks," I said. For some reason, I still wanted it wrapped around me.

Behind us the door opened. A woman came in and sat down in the back. Dale put her finger to her lips. "Let's not discuss the case," she said. "She may be a reporter. If you need to talk to Jamie or me, we can step outside."

I thought maybe it was Christine Barrett, but I couldn't be sure. She had written all those articles about Mom. She knew so much about us, and I didn't even know what she looked like.

We stood around. Jamie was trying to make small talk, but I really didn't care about the weather, or the Super Bowl. All of a sudden there were a lot of people in the room. Susan Sarsen came in and hugged us all hello, and then Faux Pa's friend Eric walked in with his wife, Amy. I'd never met Amy, but she hugged me hello anyway. She smelled good, like vanilla. Two men came forward and shook hands with Dale and Jamie. They put their stuff down on the other table. So they were the prosecutors, the lawyers for the government. I decided that I hated them.

"Come on, Leigh," Dale said. "Let's sit down."

Mom turned to Faux Pa and me and looked at us, just stared at us, for a couple seconds. Her eyes were shiny, which made me want to cry. I swallowed hard. She walked to the table and sat down in between Dale and Jamie. I took off my coat, finally, and sat with Faux Pa. Behind us Susan, Eric, and Amy had taken their seats.

Someone said, "Please rise for the Honorable Judge Barry J. Thompson." Everyone stood up. The judge came in through a door behind the bench. He sat down and told us we could be seated.

The judge wasn't at all like what I expected. He was older, like around Dr. Sherman's age, but you could tell he had been really good-looking when he was young. He had thick hair that was silver at the sides. His eyes were so blue I could see their color even from a distance. He didn't act the way judges do on TV—he didn't pound his gavel, or raise his voice. Still, I felt like I was watching some kind of show on TV. Everyone just seemed to be playing parts, including me. It didn't seem real. The judge was handsome enough to be an actor. He was wearing a black robe like judges are supposed to wear. I wondered what he had on underneath. Was he wearing a suit like the lawyers were, or was he in jeans and a T-shirt? The prosecutors each stood up and stated their names, just like they would do on a TV show: "Good afternoon, Your Honor," one of them said, the older one. "Kenneth Levine on behalf of the government." Then the younger one said, "Noah Maxwell on behalf of the government." They sat down, and Dale and Jamie stood and gave their names on behalf of the defendant, Leigh Wheeler.

There was a woman sitting in a little chair right in front of the bench, typing up everything that everyone said—the court reporter, typing up a transcript. I know it was supposed to make it official, but it just made the whole thing seem even faker, like she was typing up a TV script.

After the introductions Judge Thompson got down to business. He described what Mom had done—conspiring with Vivette and embezzling money for a period of seven and a half years. There were numbers and calculations. He said things about sentence enhancements and deductions, and he talked about some other cases. I sort of understood, but not really. I thought about the cases from American Government & Law class, like *Gideon v. Wainwright*—Gideon, who was too poor to pay for an attorney and ended up in the Supreme Court. It made me wonder if maybe one day Mom's case would be in a textbook, and students would be learning about a defendant named Wheeler.

Every so often the lawyers would say something. They always called the judge Your Honor. It made Judge Thompson seem not quite human, not like someone who would live in a house, be married, have kids, or ever have to go to the bathroom.

Mom reached up and ran her fingers through her hair. I knew she wasn't even thinking about what she was doing. I was facing the back of her head, and I saw that she had left a few strands messed up and out of place. I wanted to reach out and smooth them down, but of course I didn't. It was a weird thing to have my mother there, right in front of me, and to know I wasn't supposed to touch her.

"Mrs. Wheeler, before I formally impose a sentence, do you want to make a statement?" Judge Thompson asked.

Mom stood up. "Yes," she said.

"All right," he said. "Whenever you're ready."

"Thank you, Your Honor," Mom said. "I first want to apologize to everyone in this room." Her voice trembled. Something surged inside of me, from my stomach to my throat. My eyes started to burn. I was sure they were shiny, the way Mom's got. I blinked and blinked.

"Mrs. Wheeler, I'm sorry to interrupt you," the judge said, "but you need to speak louder for the court reporter."

Mom took a deep breath, loud enough for everyone to hear. How specific did the court reporter have to be? Did she type that part? *Defendant inhales.*

"I apologize to everyone in this room," Mom continued. "I know you are all here because of my actions, and I am deeply ashamed of the things I did to bring you here today. Over the past several months I have thought a lot about the activities I engaged in with Vivette Brooks. I want you to know that I take full responsibility for my actions. I made my own decisions, and I have no one to blame but myself. I know I abused my position at *Lovelock Falls*. I lost a job I loved; I lost the trust of my colleagues, my family, my friends, my community. I will never forgive myself, particularly for the pain this has caused my daughter. I will be sorry for that every day, for as long as I live."

Right then I wanted to tell her how sorry I was too. I was sorry for how mad I had been. It felt like the whole thing was my fault, even if that didn't make any sense. I pressed my hands together like I was praying. Maybe I was—not to God, but to Judge Thompson. *Please,* I thought. *Please don't make her go to prison. She's a good person. She's my mother.*

"I promise this court that I have learned from my mistakes," Mom continued. "I will once again be a law-abiding citizen and work to restore people's faith in me. From this moment forward I am going to dedicate my life to being someone my daughter can be proud of. Thank you."

"Thank you, Mrs. Wheeler," Judge Thompson said. "I know this is a difficult day for you and your family, and the court appreciates your candor. I will now issue my ruling."

The judge sounded like a nice person. I wondered how this could even be happening. Dale and Jamie stood up next to Mom. I stared at the back of her head. *I love you*, I thought. *Don't let this be happening.*

"It is the judgment of this court that the defendant, Leigh Catherine Wheeler, is committed to the custody of the Bureau of Prisons to be imprisoned for a term of twelve months. Mrs. Wheeler is to be housed in the northeast region of the Bureau of Prisons to facilitate visits with her family."

"Excuse me, Your Honor," the prosecutor said—the older one.

"Yes, Mr. Levine?" Judge Thompson said.

"The closest facility with availability housing inmates convicted of similar crimes to Mrs. Wheeler is in Fairlawn, West Virginia, so not in the northeast region."

"You're telling me there's not a bed in the entire Bureau of Prisons northeast region?" the judge asked.

"There is availability in the higher-security facilities, but generally the inmates are not white-collar criminals."

"Your Honor," Dale said, "I was under the impression that there was availability in Pennsylvania."

"We looked into that," Kenneth Levine said. "It is beyond capacity. We can recommend that she be moved to Pennsylvania if and when space permits."

"The West Virginia facility is Camp Petunia, correct?" Dale asked.

"That's right," Kenneth Levine said. "It's an all-women's facility."

Camp Petunia? It sounded like they were sending Mom to a summer camp for gardeners and not to a prison for white-collar criminals. It didn't make any sense.

"So be it," Judge Thompson said. "Mrs. Wheeler will be committed to the Fairlawn, West Virginia, facility, and shall be transferred to a facility in the northeast region should space become available. In addition, she is to pay restitution to her former employer in the amount of 173,200 dollars. The money must be paid back, with interest, within six months of her release from prison."

The judge paused and cleared his throat. I couldn't

imagine being a judge and sending people away from their families as part of my job. I didn't know how far away the place in West Virginia was, but I knew it had to be farther than the one in Pennsylvania—which meant driving there would take more than three hours. Maybe we'd even need to take a plane to get there. I could feel the tears starting to move silently down the sides of my face. The tear on my right cheek was moving faster than the one on my left. It made me think about gravity—something Faux Pa had taught me about a long time ago: If you drop two different things off the roof, they will both fall at the same speed. My tears were defying the law of gravity.

"Mrs. Wheeler," Judge Thompson continued, "I believe you are an intelligent person, a good person. I would advise you to make as good use of your time as you possibly can in prison. I know you will have ample time to reflect on your actions. I don't ever expect to see you in here again. Now, are there any objections to this sentence?"

"No, Your Honor," both sides said.

"Thank you," Judge Thompson said. "I hereby order the sentence to be imposed as I have stated it."

Suddenly, it was all over. The judge stood, and we all stood too. I wiped my face with the back of my hand. Dale turned around to shake Faux Pa's hand. Jamie started packing up his briefcase. The court marshal appeared to take Mom into custody. We were allowed to say good-bye first. She came out from behind the table and hugged Faux Pa, quick and hard. Then it was my turn.

I stepped toward her and fell in to her, like suddenly the muscles in my body didn't work anymore. I started crying again, out loud this time. I felt like a little kid. Mom squeezed me so tight. I didn't want her to be taken away. I was going to miss her so much. I clutched the back of her blazer, the fabric wrinkling in my fists. We were shaking from crying. There were people all around us, their voices like a buzzing sound. Right then nobody else in the world mattered. It was just Mom and me—the way it used to be. I knew I was making a memory that I would replay in my head, again and again. For the rest of my life I would remember hugging my mom right before she was handcuffed and taken away.

"I love you," Mom said, her voice thick.

"I love you too," I said. I felt like I was choking. "I love you so much."

It was probably the longest hug we had ever had. I hugged her tighter and longer than Mrs. Sarsen had, but it still ended too soon. Someone said it was time to go. I don't know who it was, but we pulled away from each other. Dale gave Mom a tissue so she could wipe her face. The court marshal brought out a pair of handcuffs. She seemed much nicer than Cruella the FBI agent, but still, she was putting handcuffs on my mother. I could almost feel the metal around my own wrists. Faux Pa was hugging me, but I just missed the way Mom's arms felt around me.

chapter twenty-two

On TV there is something that's called a montage. It's when they combine a bunch of different scenes together.

Here's an example for you: There was an episode of *Lovelock Falls* when Violet van Ryan's twin daughters were trapped in an elevator with JP Paulding, the new guy in town. He had fled to Lovelock Falls after he'd murdered his girlfriend back home, but nobody knew what he'd done, so they didn't know how dangerous he was. They showed him standing next to the twins, Gracie and Samantha. JP's hand was on the gun in his pocket. The camera cut to Violet van Ryan in a convertible, driving along the coast, her hair flying. She was laughing about something—she had no idea what was happening to her kids. And then there was Misty Briggs (obviously this was before she fell off the cliff). She had figured out the whole thing with JP

Paulding, and she was banging on the elevator doors, trying to get them to open. Because it was a montage, you knew it was all happening at the same exact moment.

Real life is like that too. You don't really think about it when you're busy living your life, but just as I was listening to Dr. Sherman drone on about the weekend homework assignment, someone else in the world was laughing at a joke, someone was crying, someone was having the best day ever, and someone was having the worst day. Mom was in prison, in Fairlawn, West Virginia. I wondered what she was doing right then. For some reason I thought about that ambulance I'd seen out of Viper's window on our way to the courthouse the day Mom was sentenced. I wondered whatever happened to the patient who was riding inside: Was he or she still alive? In pain, or all recovered? It's amazing, really, when you think of all the things that are happening in the world at the exact same time.

"Earth to Carly," Alex said.

"What?" I said.

"The bell just rang," he said.

"I know."

"You looked kinda spacey."

"Sorry," I said. "I have a lot on my mind."

"I can tell. Here." He pushed his notebook toward me. "This is what we're supposed to do by Monday. I noticed you didn't write it down."

"Thanks," I said. Alex has that boy kind of handwriting that is sometimes hard to read. I copied down what I thought it said.

He stuffed his notebook into his backpack. "All right, let's get out of here," he said. "Finally, this week is over."

We walked out of the room together. Lauren was in the hallway by her locker.

"How was science?" she asked.

"Very scientific," Alex said. "Ask Carly—she was really into it today."

"Yeah, right," I said.

Alex grinned his butter-melting grin. "So Laur, are you up for a movie this weekend?"

Alex and Lauren had sort of started dating. They didn't hang out together in school that much, and they didn't call each other boyfriend and girlfriend, but everyone knew that's what they were. Jordan told me they had kissed at Annie's party. For some reason Annie was still speaking to Lauren. I didn't know why—but with everything going on with Mom, and my not being friends with Annie anymore, I felt out of the loop. I guess it just proved that the real reason Annie didn't want to be friends with me had nothing to do with Alex.

"I'll try," Lauren said. "If I can escape my parents' study schedule."

"Cool," Alex said. "I gotta go. I'm meeting Nate, but I'll call you later."

"See you," Lauren said.

"Give me a hug," Alex said. He opened up his arms and Lauren hugged him back. When they pulled away from each other, he said, "You too, Carly." I was surprised he wanted to hug me. Hugs are a big thing at Preston. We always hug each other good-bye, but usually it's just girls hugging other girls, like hugs of friendship. I stepped toward him, and Alex gave me a quick hug. "Hope you have an excellent weekend," he said.

"Thanks," I said. We watched him walk down the

hall and turn at the corner. "He's nice," I told Lauren. "You're lucky."

"I know," she said. "But I think the only reason he wanted to hug me was to see if I was wearing a bra."

"Seriously?"

"Yup," she said, shaking her head. "He sort of moved his hand up and down my back. Totally childish."

Lauren was smiling, so I knew she didn't really mind. Alex hadn't rubbed his hand up and down my back. I wondered if it was because he already knew I wasn't wearing a bra. I remembered how at camp last summer this girl Erin went to snap my bra, and I was so embarrassed because of course there was nothing there.

"I guess I won't have to worry about that for a while," I told Lauren. "I'm still completely flat."

"Not completely," Lauren said. "You're like the size I was when I first started to wear a bra—you know, like a training bra."

"No I'm not," I said. I crossed my arms in front of my chest, but really I wanted to look down and see what Lauren saw. Of course I didn't; it would be totally weird to stand in the hallway checking myself out. "I have to get my French book from my locker before I get on the bus," I told her.

"Okay," she said. "What are you doing this weekend?"

I shrugged. I used to have plans with friends on the weekends. I used to have a much busier social life. "Jessa and Justin will be over. I'm not sure what my stepfather has planned."

"Have fun, whatever you do," she said.

"Thanks," I said. I headed over to my locker, packed up the books I would need for the next two days, and walked outside to the bus line.

Faux Pa is usually home Friday afternoons, but when I got home that day there was a note in the foyer: *C, Running errands and then picking up Jessa & Justin. Will be home by 6. Love, FP.* I was relieved he wasn't there, because that meant I could go straight upstairs without him asking any questions. I went to my room, closed the door, dumped my backpack on the floor, and took off my shirt. There's a full-length mirror on the back of the door, and I stood in front of it.

There they were: I had boobs. Not big ones, but still. My nipples were popping out. It was like they were little buds that had sprouted overnight. The right one seemed just a little bit larger than the left, and I hoped it wouldn't stay that way. But whatever happened, I was officially no longer flat-chested. I stared at my chest for so long that it seemed to not even be a part of me.

It had only been eleven days since Mom had gone away. How was it possible that my body had changed so quickly? It was nice to finally have a reason to wear a bra, but now I had a bigger problem. I hadn't let Mom take me shopping for bras when she was still home, and she was going to be gone for a year. It wasn't the kind of thing I could really talk to Faux Pa about.

I couldn't even call Mom, because prisoners aren't allowed to receive phone calls. Eventually she would be able to make them, but the lawyers said it would be a couple more weeks before it was all set up, and even then there would be a lot of rules. She'd have to use a pay phone and call us collect, and she'd only be allowed to stay on for a few minutes each time. The calls would be monitored, also, which meant someone from the prison would be listening in on everything we said. I couldn't imagine talking to Mom about needing a bra, knowing someone could hear me.

Life is a montage, I thought. *Right now I'm picking up my shirt and putting it back on, and at this exact same moment Mom is in prison. She has no idea that this is happening, that my body is changing, and that I really need her.*

chapter twenty-three

On Saturday I was sitting in my room, missing Mom and feeling angry at her at the same time, when someone knocked on my bedroom door. "Come in," I said. I expected it to be Faux Pa, but there was Jessa in her black leggings and black cardigan sweater. We'd never had a hanging-out kind of relationship, so it was weird when she walked in and sat down on the edge of the bed.

"I just wanted to check on you," she said.

"I'm okay," I told her.

"Good," she said. She held up her arm and pulled a piece of lint off the sleeve of her sweater. "You know, it's sort of weird that you're living alone with my dad. I can't imagine doing that. I haven't lived with him full-time in seven years."

"Yeah," I said, "but I'm used to living with him."

Jessa nodded. "I guess you would be," she said. For a second I wondered if she was mad that I was used to living with Faux Pa when she only got to live with him every other weekend, but then she continued. "Just so you know, you can tell me if you ever need anything. I know sometimes it's hard to talk to my dad about things—at least it is for me."

It was like Jessa had a sixth sense, and I felt my face flush. I did need something. It had never occurred to me to go to Jessa about it, but it was better than having to ask Faux Pa, or waiting until Mom got home.

Jessa must have noticed that I was blushing. "Tell me," she said.

"This is totally embarrassing," I said.

"Knowing you, I really doubt it's anything too bad," she said.

Knowing me? I didn't think Jessa knew me that well at all. Then again, we'd been stepsisters for five years. She must know some things about me. I pressed my palms against my eyes. "I think I need a bra," I said.

Jessa leaned forward and pulled my hands away from my face. She was smiling. "That is so not a big deal," she said.

"It is when it's your first!" I said. I mean, it was supposed to be, wasn't it? I should've had my mom at home to get all excited and plan a shopping trip. Instead, I felt stressed out and miserable.

"Not what I meant," Jessa said. "It's just nothing to be embarrassed about. I'm actually surprised you don't have one already—or have, like, twenty. You and Leigh were always shopping."

"We didn't shop for bras," I said. "I never needed one before."

"Sometimes I wish that was my problem," Jessa said. "Bras are a pain. They can be uncomfortable, and you have to make sure you remember not to wear a black bra under a white T-shirt, or else everyone will just stare at your chest the whole day." I couldn't remember the last time I'd seen Jessa wearing a white shirt. Maybe that was part of the reason she liked black so much, so no one could see her bra.

"Yeah, well, I still have to get one," I said.

Jessa looked at me—not at my face, but at my chest. It made me so self-conscious. "It's not like an emergency situation," she said. "You're not hanging out all over the place or anything."

I knew she was right. I didn't *need* a bra. But now that I finally had a little something to put in one, I really wanted to have one.

"You know," Jessa said, "we should go shopping this weekend."

"Really?"

"Sure, why not?"

"Cool," I said. "Thanks."

"I'll tell my dad to drive us to the mall. I'm sure he'll be happy that we're bonding."

"Just don't tell your dad what we're going to buy," I said.

"Don't worry," Jessa said. "I'm good at keeping things to myself."

We ended up going to the big mall in White Plains on Sunday. Faux Pa told Jessa we shouldn't be spending any money, but Jessa said she had Christmas money and she wanted to go shopping. Faux Pa dropped us off and then took Justin to his hockey game.

I've always felt completely at home in malls—

particularly in department stores—I guess because I spent so much time shopping with Mom. There's just something about the way a department store is set up. I can sense where to find things. I like trying on clothes and modeling in front of dressing room mirrors. Mom would get excited whenever we found something that fit me really well. Clothes just made her happy.

But Mom wasn't there, Jessa wasn't as into clothing as I was, and of course I'd never shopped for bras before. It was like going home and discovering things were out of place. Jessa and I walked into Nordstrom, one of the department stores in the mall. "I usually shop in vintage places," she explained. "But it's kind of gross to get used bras. I only really come here for bras and underwear."

We took the escalator up to the third floor, where the lingerie was. Racks and racks of bras and underpants in all different styles, fabrics, and colors. There were even wild patterns, like zebra print and polka dots. Usually, I like to have a lot of choices when I'm shopping, but right then I felt overwhelmed. A man walked by us, and I wanted to tell Jessa we could forget the whole thing—the last thing I wanted was to have a guy watch me shop for bras. My boobs weren't that big. Maybe I could wait for Mom after all.

Just then one of the saleswomen came over to us. "Can I help you with anything?" she asked.

We were in the bra department, so it was obvious we were shopping for bras. But still, I felt funny saying it out loud. I turned to Jessa. "We're okay on our own," Jessa said.

"You're sisters, right?" the saleswoman asked. She was kind of hovering over us.

"Yeah," Jessa said.

The woman nodded. "I could see it in your eyes," she said. "You both have beautiful eyes."

"Thanks," Jessa said. She didn't tell her we had completely different parents, and I was glad. I kind of liked looking like Jessa's sister.

"If you need anything, I'm here to help," she continued. "My name is Bobbi."

"Okay, thanks," Jessa said. She turned away from Bobbi. Mom always made friends with the saleswomen, but clearly that wasn't Jessa's style. She pulled me toward the back, to a wall of bras. Some of the cups were so big I thought I could probably fit my head into them. "We're better off alone," Jessa told me. "When Reese and I went bra shopping a couple months ago, the saleswoman barged into the dressing room without even knocking. Besides, I have a lot of experience with bras. Here, what about this one?"

She pulled a little white bra down from the rack on the wall. I touched it to feel the fabric, the way Mom always did. I rubbed it between my fingers. It was soft and stretchy. "It doesn't have the wires in it," I said. "Doesn't that make you saggy?"

Jessa smiled. "You don't need underwire—at least not yet."

"I guess it's okay then," I said. "It feels like it will be comfortable."

"That's important," Jessa said. "It sucks when you get one that's just a little bit itchy. You think it will be okay, but the longer you wear it, the worse it gets. Go try it on, and I'll try and find a few more options."

When I was little and played dress-up with Mom's clothes, sometimes I put on her bras, stuffing socks into the cups so they'd be all filled out. Now when I went into the dressing room and took off my shirt, it kind of felt like I was playing dress-up again, like the bra didn't really belong on me. I put my arms through the straps and reached back to hook the two sides together, but it wasn't working. Then I remembered how Mom put on her bra, hooking the back part in the front and then twisting the whole thing around before she put her arms through the straps. I did it that way and looked in the mirror.

It was a little too big—not the cups, but just loose all around, and I felt like my body was swimming under the fabric. I put my shirt on again and went back to Jessa. She handed me a few other bras, and I headed back into the dressing room.

I knew if Mom had been there, she would have come in with me, but Jessa waited in the hall outside the dressing room. The first couple of styles I tried on weren't quite right, but finally I found a light pink one that fit—it was plain cotton, like the fabric of an undershirt. The triangles covered me up enough. There was even room for me to grow into it a little more. I put my shirt on over it, just to see what it would be like. You couldn't really tell that I was wearing a bra, but I rubbed my fingers along the bra straps, liking the way they felt. I felt older, somehow.

I took it off again and brought it out to Jessa. I was a little embarrassed to just be carrying it out in the open like that. I guess it's something you get used to when you've shopped for bras a few times. Jessa said it came in other colors, and she thought I should get three of them. "It's not like underwear," Jessa explained. "You don't have to wash your bra every time you wear it, so three is a perfect amount."

I turned the bra over and looked at the price tag. Twenty-five dollars. I hadn't realized a little piece of fabric would cost so much. It was stupid of me, because I knew clothing could be expensive, but it's not like it was a designer label; at least I didn't think so. I guess I didn't know enough about bras to know what the expensive brands were. I just knew I didn't have enough money to buy three of them. One would have to be enough.

"I'll just start with this one," I said.

"Why?" Jessa asked. "You need to have at least one white bra. That way you can wear it with anything. Besides, you're not going to want to wear the same bra every day."

"I didn't realize how expensive bras were," I said.

"Don't worry about it," Jessa said. "I have money for the other two."

She went to get my bra in a couple more colors—a white one and a yellow one—and then she motioned for me to follow her to the cash register. "You really don't have to do this," I said. "It's my fault for not telling Faux Pa—I mean, your dad. He would've given me money if he knew I needed bras."

At least I thought he would've given me the money. I knew he was worried about spending too much, but bras were important. It wasn't like I was shopping for makeup or shoes I didn't need. The truth was, I'd never thought about the things I could or couldn't ask Faux Pa for, because I'd always had Mom.

"It's okay," Jessa said. "I really do have my Christmas money with me, and some babysitting money too."

"I can't believe you're using your Christmas money on me," I said. "I'll pay you back one day."

Jessa shook her head. "I want to do this," she said. "Think of it this way—I was being honest with my dad about spending my Christmas money."

I watched Bobbi ring up the bras. Jessa handed over the money, and Bobbi gave her change. Then she wrapped the bras up in tissue paper, folding them so gently, as if they would break, and put them into a shopping bag. I paid for the pink one myself. "You can put it in the same bag," I told Bobbi.

"Congratulations on your first bras," Jessa said.

"Thanks," I said. I was blushing again.

"And now you'll be wearing one for the rest of your life."

Jessa said we should buy a T-shirt or a sweater so if Faux Pa and Justin asked to see what we'd gotten, we could show it to them and leave the bras buried in the bottom of the bag. I felt bad about her having to spend more money, but she said she would just come back the next weekend with her mom and return it. Right then she really felt like my sister. I felt like she was taking me seriously.

Faux Pa always said that Jessa went through phases—her "Daddy's girl" phase when she was really little, her moody phase in middle school, and her "dark and mysterious" phase once she hit high school. Now it seemed like Jessa was going through a new phase—a "let's be sisters" phase. I hoped her new phase would last a while—at least until Mom got back. Maybe it wouldn't even be a phase. Maybe we were both growing up.

The teen department is right across from the lingerie department. Jessa walked over to a table of long-sleeved T-shirts. "You should get the blue one," I told her. "It matches your eyes." I knew it didn't matter, since she'd be returning anyway, but she brought it up to the register.

Afterward we walked out of Nordstrom and went into a couple other stores, just to window-shop. Faux Pa called Jessa's cell phone to say Justin's game was over and they were on their way. He said we should meet them for lunch at the Cheesecake Factory. Jessa and I headed to Neiman Marcus, because the best way to get to the restaurant was to walk through the store and then cross the street. I knew that from when I shopped with Mom. Neiman Marcus is the most expensive department store in the mall and Mom's favorite. Faux Pa made fun of it—he called it "Needless Markup." But Jessa and I weren't going to do any shopping there. We were just passing through.

There was a woman handing out flyers as we were walking out the door. Jessa shook her head as she passed her, but I felt bad not taking one. "Thanks," I said. I glanced down at it, and there was Ally's face staring back at me. NEIMAN MARCUS WELCOMES VIOLET VAN RYAN OF "LOVELOCK FALLS," the flyer read. It went on to give details about when Ally would be there—on a Saturday in a couple of weeks. Apparently, she would be promoting some perfume that her character supposedly wore on the show. Customers could try out the perfume and meet Ally.

Sometimes I felt like *Lovelock Falls* was following me—it had been on TV when Mom and I went to visit Grandma, and it was always on my mind. Now this. I wondered if the flyer was some kind of sign. I hadn't been shopping in months, and now the first time I was back at the mall, someone handed me a piece of paper with Ally's picture on it.

Then again, it could just be a coincidence. *Lovelock*

Falls was a popular show, and Ally Jaron was the star. It didn't have to mean anything.

I folded up the flyer and stuffed it into the back pocket of my jeans. Jessa and I walked into the restaurant, past the host desk toward the tables in the back. The restaurant was crowded and noisy, which made it harder. "Carly! Jess!" Faux Pa called. I turned in the direction of his voice. There he was, sitting in a big booth with Justin. A woman was sitting on the other side of Justin. I was so surprised to see her there that it took me a couple seconds to figure out that it was Jocelyn.

"Mom, what are you doing here?" Jessa asked.

"I was at Justin's game, and he wanted me to come for lunch," Jocelyn said.

"It's cool that you're here," Jessa said. She sat down next to Jocelyn.

"Carly, come sit," Faux Pa said. "How was shopping?"

"Good," I said.

"What did you get?"

"Nothing," I said. "Jessa got a blue shirt."

"Really," Faux Pa said. "Not black?"

"Carly picked it out," Jessa said.

"I like the way you look in blue," Jocelyn said. She ran her fingers through Jessa's hair. It was such a normal, motherly gesture, and it made me jealous—Jessa got to be with her mother.

"Girls, I ordered a few things to share," Faux Pa said. "Chicken and a pasta dish, and one of the big salads."

"And I got my own order of buffalo wings," Justin said.

"Right, and Justin got the buffalo wings appetizer, so you can taste those, too."

"But I shouldn't have to share, because that's all I'm gonna eat," Justin said.

"Oh, no," Jocelyn said. "You're going to eat some salad, too."

Justin looked to Faux Pa for support. "Dad, I don't really have to eat salad, do I?"

"Yes," Faux Pa said. "Listen to your mother."

It seemed so natural the way he said it. I sat there and just stared at them: the four *J*s. Mom was away, and they were reunited. Justin didn't seem uncomfortable or shy, the way he is with Mom sometimes. All morning Jessa had seemed like my sister, but now I felt like I didn't belong. I was as confused as ever.

chapter twenty-four

It was raining the next Saturday—raining again, which fit my mood. I felt dark and dreary. Jessa and Justin were with Jocelyn, and Faux Pa sat me down to talk about money.

He said we were going to have to make some tough choices—there was a possibility that I'd have to leave Preston after the end of the year and go to the public school in the fall. I had been at Preston since kindergarten, and it was hard to imagine it not being my school, but there was a part of me that thought maybe it would be easier. I could walk to school, Amelia went there, and I wouldn't have to see Annie anymore. Faux Pa explained that he was going to meet with Mrs. Gilbert, the head of Preston, to see if they would give me a scholarship for next year. He said nothing was written in stone, but he just wanted to prepare me for having to make a change. And then he told me the really awful thing: He had put our house up for sale.

"I've gone over the numbers," he said. "It's just too hard to keep this house. Mom's not working anymore, so we only have my income to live off of, and when she comes home, we'll have to pay back the money to *Lovelock Falls*."

"It's not fair," I said. I had been sitting there quietly, just listening and feeling sort of numb. But when he said the part about my house, the numbness wore off. "I didn't do anything wrong, and it's like I keep getting punished."

"I'm sorry, honey," Faux Pa said. "I don't want to move either, but we need the money."

"We also need a place to live," I reminded him. "How is it saving money if we just have to buy another house?"

"We may rent something instead of buying right now," Faux Pa said. "And we'll move into something smaller. We won't go too far, so we'll remain in this school district. If you have to go to public school, you'll be with Amelia."

"When will we move?"

"It depends on how long it takes to sell our place," he said. "I don't know how long that will be. In the meantime I just wanted to get an idea of what's out there."

He told me he'd seen an open house for an apartment advertised in the paper that morning, and he wanted us to go. I went up to my room to get dressed. I sat down on my bed as I was putting on my shoes. I was thinking about all the times Mom had come in to say good night. I wondered how long it would take to sell our house. A month or two? Six months? Probably not a whole year, which meant Mom would never see my room again. She would never walk in my door at this house, pad across my pink rug with the diamond pattern, and sit on my bed by the window. I would have a different room in a different home. My heart was racing just from thinking about it.

I realized that I had stopped imagining disasters; my head was full of the bad stuff that was really happening to me.

Faux Pa drove us over to see the apartment from the newspaper. It was just about ten minutes from our house. The building had a circular driveway, but you weren't allowed to park there. It was just for picking up and dropping off. We parked on the street and walked up the driveway into the building. There was a sign in the lobby directing us to the right apartment. Faux Pa and I got off the elevator and walked down a narrow hallway. All the doors were painted the same color—light blue—and I wondered if people sometimes walked into the wrong apartments. The door to apartment 4B was open. "Here we are, Car," Faux Pa said. I let him walk in first and followed behind him.

The realtor came up and introduced herself to Faux Pa and me. She told us to feel free to explore the apartment. We walked around. It didn't take very long. There was a common room that was like a combination living room/den/dining room. The kitchen was the smallest kitchen I'd ever seen. We walked down a hallway, passing a couple bathrooms, to the bedrooms—two smallish bedrooms and one that was so tiny I wondered how any furniture could even fit inside.

If Mom had been there, I bet she would have made a joke about how Faux Pa wouldn't have to worry about our decibel levels in an apartment so small—there would be no need to shout up the stairs. I could hear footsteps from the people living in the apartment above. I knew that would bother me if we moved in. It would feel like having strangers living with us all the time. *Plenty of kids have to live in apartments instead of houses*, I reminded myself. But there was something so much worse about the way it was happening to me. I just think it's harder to live in an apartment after you've spent the first nearly thirteen years of your life in a house.

On the way home it started snowing a little, but not the good kind of snow that sticks to the ground and looks pretty—just these heavy, wet flakes. Faux Pa parked the car. Outside, it was quiet, the way it is in winter. I looked over at Amelia's house. We had lived across from each other our whole lives. I didn't want to go to school with her; I wanted to live across the street from her, the way I always had. I wanted things to go back to normal, and I knew they never would.

We walked up the driveway: our driveway, that we could just park in, because it was our house and we didn't have to share it with anyone. I was feeling selfish and spoiled and mad. I wanted to go up to my room and wallow in my misery, but Faux Pa told me to sit with him in the den. I didn't know why, since we weren't really talking to each other. I sat on the couch and kicked off my shoes. They each landed with a thud. If we were in an apartment, would the people below be able to hear the thuds when I kicked off my shoes?

My eyes moved around the room. I was noticing

everything more because I was thinking of having to live without it—or, actually, I was thinking about having to set it up in another home, and how it would look all wrong. There was the media stand and the TV and the coffee table and the matching lamps on either side of the couch. The only things missing were the framed certificates that used to be on the walls, from when Mom was nominated for awards for being a stylist on *Lovelock Falls*. I wondered what had happened to them—did she box them up, or were they thrown away? But there was the striped rug, and the chair with the stain on it from when I'd spilled orange juice. Mom had been looking for new fabric to reupholster the chair, but then she was arrested. At some point she covered the stain with an afghan Grandma had made.

Everything fit into the room just right. I'd never noticed it before. I'd always taken everything about my house for granted. You don't think about how much you need your house when you're busy living in it. But our house seemed like a part of our family. It was hard to imagine living anywhere else, having our stuff set up in a completely different place.

Mom, this is all your fault! I thought.

The phone rang suddenly. For nineteen days—ever since the sentencing—whenever the phone rang, I hoped it would be Mom. We were still waiting for her to get her phone privileges. It was like she was a little kid and she couldn't use the phone until she had permission. I had wanted to be the one to answer the phone the first time she called, but now I was mad at her all over again.

I watched Faux Pa reach for the phone. He checked

the caller ID and turned to me. "Do you know a Daniel Ross?"

"That's Jordan's dad's name," I said. Jordan hadn't called me in weeks. It was just the way things were now. Faux Pa handed me the receiver, and I pressed the talk button, even though I wondered if Jordan had dialed my house by mistake, or if maybe she somehow knew that I might not be back at Preston next year and she was calling to find out all the gossip about it. Thinking that made me almost happy to maybe be leaving. "Hello?" I said.

"Hey, Carly," Jordan said, "did you hear?" Her voice sounded breathy and excited.

"Hear what?" I asked.

"Annie's mom was sent to prison last night."

"What?" I asked. "What are you talking about?" I sat forward and pressed the phone harder to my ear, in case I just hadn't heard right.

"She was making a turn off of Central Avenue, and her car skidded, I guess because of the weather. The cops showed up and arrested her for drinking and driving."

"But she never drives herself," I said. "She has Gerry—the driver."

"Maybe Gerry was sick or something," Jordan said. "Anyway, she was drunk, and they took her in. She's not going to be able to get out of prison until Monday."

"Jail," I said. "Prison is long-term, and jail is just for a few days."

"Oh," Jordan said, "whatever."

I wished I hadn't said that. I didn't want to be known as the prison expert, even though I guessed I sort of was.

"How do you know all this?" I asked.

"My dad's friend Donnie is really tight with Annie's dad," Jordan explained. "When Mrs. Rothschild was arrested, she was allowed to call someone, but Annie's dad wasn't picking up the phone, so she ended up calling Donnie. He told my dad."

If you asked me, it was pretty awful of Donnie to blab about the whole thing to Jordan's dad.

"I just thought you should know," Jordan said. "I mean, seriously, can you believe it?"

"No," I said. My head was spinning. The whole thing was crazy. Everything about the day seemed unreal—Faux Pa having to sell our house, and Annie's mom being arrested, and the fact that my mom was sitting in prison and I wasn't even able to talk to her.

"I wonder what will happen to her mom," Jordan said. "Like, maybe she'll have to go back to jail for a long time." I didn't bother to explain that if she went back, it would probably be to a prison. "I called Annie, but she said she couldn't talk. She must feel so bad—about you, I mean."

"I don't know," I said.

"Driving drunk is really awful," Jordan continued. "Your mom never did anything like that."

"No, she didn't," I said.

Mom might have used money that wasn't hers, but Mrs. Rothschild could've hit another car and hurt someone. She could've even killed someone. And yet we were the ones who were going to have to sell our house, and they were still in their mansion. It didn't seem right. It didn't seem fair. Right then I remembered what Lauren had said: *People in glass houses shouldn't throw stones*. I realized what she had meant: You shouldn't judge people for having the same faults that you have yourself.

I didn't want to stay on the phone and gossip about Annie. I guess you would think that being the subject of all the gossip would make me really excited about finally getting to talk about someone else's problems, but it was the opposite, really.

"I actually have to go," I told Jordan. "I was in the middle of something with my stepfather."

"No problem," Jordan said. "I'll call you later if Annie calls me back."

We said good-bye. I pressed the off button and watched the keypad go dark. "You didn't have to hang up for me," Faux Pa said.

"I wanted to get off the phone," I told him.

"Is everything okay?"

"Not really," I said. I felt like I was going to cry, but I wasn't sure why. Was it because of the house, or because of Annie? "I really wish Mom was here."

Faux Pa picked up my hand and squeezed it. "What happened, baby?"

"Annie's mom was arrested for drunk driving," I said.

"That's what Jordan called to tell you?"

I nodded. "Annie and I aren't even friends any-more. Her parents don't want her to hang out with me because of Mom."

"She could probably use a friend like you right now," Faux Pa said.

I thought about the way Mrs. Sarsen had hugged Mom. "Yeah, maybe," I said. "I guess I could call her, but what if her dad answers the phone and he gets mad at me?"

"If Carson Rothschild gets angry that you're calling Annie, then you can give me the phone and I'll give him a piece of my mind," Faux Pa said. He was so stern that I had to smile.

"What if Annie just doesn't want to talk to me?"

"Well then, Carly, you can hang up the phone knowing you did the right thing."

I went up to my room so I could call Annie in private. My heart was pounding; it felt like a warning, like it was a mistake to call her. *There's no such thing as a mistake*, I told myself. I picked up the phone and dialed Annie's number—her cell phone number, because then at least her dad wouldn't answer.

It rang once, twice. If Annie didn't pick up, I decided I would just hang up. I didn't want to leave a message. We have a blocked phone number, so she'd never know it was me. "Hello?"

"Annie?"

"Yes?"

"It's Carly," I said.

"I know your voice," she said coolly.

"I heard about your mom," I said. "Jordan just called me."

"And I guess you're calling to rub it in," she said.

"No," I said. "I just wanted to see how you are."

"Obviously, I'm great. I'm the best ever," Annie said, her voice cracking on the last word. Hearing her like that made something rise up inside of me. Annie isn't a crier. In all the years we'd been friends, I'd barely ever seen her cry.

I took a deep breath. "I'm really sorry," I said.

"Sorry for what?" Annie snapped. "That my mom drinks too much, or that she's locked up now?"

"I'm sorry for everything," I said.

"Why are you being so nice to me?"

"Because I know how it feels," I said. "It just sucks."

She didn't say anything right away. I heard her on the other end of the phone, breathing deeply, her breath catching—the sounds you make when you're trying to keep yourself from crying, or trying to stop crying. "It really does," Annie said finally. "I can't believe this is happening. I never thought this would happen to me."

"Me either," I said. "At least your mom didn't get hurt."

"Yeah," Annie said. "That's what everyone keeps saying. I just know she must be going crazy right now. You know how she is—always wanting to keep up appearances and pretend we're a perfect family. I guess she won't be able to do that anymore. Everyone's going to know about it."

"You'll find out who your true friends are," I said. There was silence on the other end of the phone. "Are you still there?" I asked finally.

"Yeah, I'm here," Annie said. "I know I was a bad friend. A *seriously* bad friend. My mom was saying all these things. Usually, I don't even listen to her, but it was all so weird. I didn't know what to think about it. And then there was Alex Jedder."

"Alex and I are just friends," I told her, as emphatically as I could. "I swear that's it."

"I know," she said. "It was stupid. I don't even like him anymore. I danced with Trevor Christopher at my birthday party."

"Really?" I asked. It was weird to hear something like that, weeks after it had happened.

"Yeah," Annie said. "None of it matters now, though. My dad goes crazy every time the phone rings because he thinks it might be a reporter. My mom hasn't been in the news yet, but she probably will, because of who my dad is."

"I thought maybe you wouldn't answer the phone, or that you'd hang up on me when you heard it was me calling."

"I figured the reporters wouldn't call on my cell," Annie said. "I thought about hanging up when I heard your voice, but I sort of wanted to talk to you."

"I've wanted to talk to you, too," I said. "For a long time I've wanted to."

"So my mom had to get arrested for us to talk," Annie said. "That's kind of messed up, you know."

"Yeah, well, whatever it takes," I said.

"We both have mothers in jail right now," Annie said. "Can you believe it?"

I decided not to correct her on the jail-versus-prison thing. I wanted to say something to lighten the mood, to make it seem like things would be okay. All of a sudden I broke into my commercial announcer's voice: "Is your mother in prison? Are you worried about reporters calling your house? Well, you need the Phone Scrambler. Just attach it to your phone. It has special radar to sense when a reporter is calling, and it will automatically disconnect the call."

"If you buy now," Annie said, "we'll upgrade your order to the Turbo Phone Scrambler for no extra cost—the reporter who tried to call you will never be able to make a phone call, ever again!"

"Quantities are limited," I said. "So act now."

Annie started laughing, and I laughed too, just like we used to laugh together. "Listen," she said, "I hear my dad calling me, so I have to go. But I'll call you later."

"Okay," I said.

"Really, I will," she said.

"Okay," I said again. We said good-bye. I waited until I heard the click on her end, and then I pressed the off button on the phone.

chapter twenty-five

The next week, finally, Mom called. I answered the phone, and there was a recorded voice saying I was receiving a call from an inmate in a federal prison.

It had been twenty-three days since Mom's sentencing—twenty-three days since I had seen her or heard her voice. It was almost a whole month. She was calling collect, so I had to agree to accept the charges. "Mom?" I said.

"Carly," Mom said, "you have no idea how much I've missed just hearing your voice."

My chest was tight, and it was hard to talk. "Me too," I said. It came out like kind of a whisper, not my regular voice—it seemed kind of ironic, since that's what Mom missed hearing. We were both quiet for a couple seconds. I listened to her breathe through the phone. I wished there were a way to just have an open phone line for the whole time Mom was in prison, or maybe walkie-talkies that we could each have. That way if I ever needed her, I could press a button, and she would be there. They should invent that for kids whose parents are in prison.

"Honey," Mom said, "I'm sorry this is hard, but I don't want to waste all our time. I only get a few minutes on the phone."

"I know," I said. Dale had told us that Mom's phone conversations would be limited, but I didn't really know what we should be talking about. It was weird not to know what to say to my own mother. "How are you?" I asked.

"I'm all right," she said. "I have a cold, so it's a little hard to breathe. I've been breathing all my life—you'd think I'd be better at it."

"Is there a doctor there?" I asked. "Maybe you need one of those inhalers."

"I was kidding, honey," Mom said. "It's just a cold. You had a cold a couple months ago and you recovered. I'll be fine. I'm already better than I was yesterday. I was able to go to work today."

"You're working?" I asked.

"Everyone has to work here," Mom said. "It breaks up the day, so I don't really mind it. I work in the kitchen."

She went on a little bit about her job and the people she was meeting. She said the prison was crowded, and there were all sorts of people, convicted of all sorts of crimes. It was so strange. Usually when I'm on the phone with someone, I get an idea in my head of what it looks like. Like when I'm on the phone with Annie, I can see her in her room, lying on her bed with the celadon-green toile comforter. But I couldn't picture where Mom was at all. It made her seem even farther away. She could've been calling from the moon.

"Tell me about what's been going on in your life," Mom said.

I didn't really know where to begin. She had missed so much, and I knew I couldn't fill her in on everything when we only had a few minutes on the phone. Besides, most mothers are just there when things happen, so they know what's going on in your life.

"I don't know," I said. "Nothing much."

The recorded voice came back on the line, warning that the conversation had almost reached the time limit and was about to be terminated. "Mom, are you still there?"

"I'm still here," she said. "I guess we have to wrap this up. Tell Faux Pa I'll speak to him the next time I call, and please have him take you to visit Grandma sometime in the next few days."

"She doesn't even know who I am," I reminded her.

"I know," Mom said. "But it would mean a lot to me since I can't get there."

I hated that she said that—it made me feel guilty, even though it was her fault that she couldn't visit Grandma herself. I wondered if I would ever be able to talk to Mom and not find a reason to be mad.

"I'll call you again as soon as I can," Mom said.

"When will that be?" I asked.

She started to say something, but the line went dead. I held the receiver in my hand for a few seconds, just staring at it, before I finally hung it up.

chapter twenty-six

Faux Pa and I went to visit Grandma after school on Friday. He picked me up, so I didn't have to take the bus home, and we drove up to the nursing home.

I couldn't remember the last time Faux Pa had come to visit Grandma. By the time he married Mom, Grandma was already so forgetful. She never really knew who he was.

I could hear Grandma's TV blaring from the hallway. When we got to her room, she was sitting up in bed, but her eyes were closed. One of those courtroom shows was on TV. I was glad it was too late for *Lovelock Falls* to be on. Ally Jaron would be at Neiman Marcus the next day—that perfume promotional event. I knew the lay-out of the store so well, and I could picture her sitting in the cosmetics area with people all around her. I real-ized that Grandma probably couldn't do that—picture a place in her head, like the mall. It made me wonder what you think about when you don't remember things.

"Order in the court!" the judge on the screen yelled.

It was amazing that Grandma could actually sleep through the noise. Faux Pa and I stood in the doorway for a few seconds, unsure of what to do. "Let's take a walk," he suggested. "We'll come back in a few minutes."

I hated walking around the nursing home. It smelled like antiseptic, and there were all those old people looking at me. I wondered what they thought of me—did they like seeing kids in the halls, or did it remind them that they weren't young anymore? "Fine," I said.

"I'll just turn the TV down so the entire floor doesn't have to hear it," he said.

He crossed the room and picked up the remote from Grandma's bedside table. She opened her eyes and grabbed his wrist. Her eyes looked so old. They were ringed with red, and the skin around them was papery, like it could tear. She glared at Faux Pa. "Watch yourself, buster," Grandma said. "Where do you think you're going with that?"

Faux Pa jumped back, like he was afraid, but he smiled. "Hi, Gwen," he said.

"How do you know my name?" Grandma asked him, sounding accusatory.

"I'm married to Leigh," he told her.

"Leigh who?" Grandma asked.

I felt a chill right then—Grandma had forgotten Mom, her own daughter. I knew it was because of the Alzheimer's, but still. It was just so sad.

"Leigh is your daughter," Faux Pa told her. "And Carly is her daughter—your granddaughter. We came to see you."

"Hi, Grandma," I said. I stepped farther into the room.

"All these people," Grandma said. "I can't keep up with all these people. Well, I hope you ate before you came, because I only cooked enough for me and the boys, and it's too late now to buy any more food."

"Don't worry, Gwen," Faux Pa said. "We just came by to say hello. Is it all right if we sit down and talk for a few minutes?"

"I have to watch TV," Grandma said.

"We can watch with you," Faux Pa said.

"Suit yourself," Grandma told him.

We sat down in the visitor chairs. Faux Pa is so tall that even when he's sitting down, he looks tall. The judge on the screen didn't sound anything like Judge Thompson. He seemed gruff and abrasive, not at all professional. I listened to him tell the lawyers they were idiots. Then he told the defendant that he was an idiot. "You may be the most idiotic bunch to ever grace this courtroom," the judge said. It was strange to know that wasn't how judges really acted—at least not how they acted when the cameras weren't on. They just made it more dramatic for television.

Faux Pa and I stayed until the show was over, and then he said we should go pick up Jessa and Justin for the weekend. "It was good to see you," Faux Pa told Grandma. "We'll come back soon."

"Bye, Grandma," I said. "Mom says she's thinking about you."

"Who did you say your mom was?" Grandma asked.

"Leigh," I said. "Your daughter."

"Yes, that's right," Grandma said. "She came to visit me this morning, but she forgot the Fritos."

Some things were just easier for Grandma. She didn't have a sense of what happened on what day.

She didn't remember enough to have to miss things. "I'll bring you Fritos next time I come," I said.

"I'll hold you to it," Grandma said. I think she may have winked at me. Then she turned back to the TV, and we were strangers again.

Faux Pa and I rode the elevator downstairs. The nurse, Carol, was in the lobby, and she called out to me as I followed Faux Pa to the front door.

"Hi," I said. Faux Pa introduced himself and shook Carol's hand.

"Give your mom my best," Carol said.

I nodded. I wondered if she said that because she knew where Mom was, or just because she liked Mom and hadn't seen her in a few weeks. We said good-bye. Faux Pa and I walked out of the building. As we crossed the parking lot to the car, he pulled his phone out of his pocket and called Jessa and Justin. I could tell it was Jocelyn who answered the phone. "Tell the kids I'm on my way," Faux Pa said. "Yup, I'll see you soon."

In the past when I'd gone with Faux Pa to pick up Jessa and Justin, we'd stayed in the car and they'd come out to meet us. We never saw Jocelyn. What did it mean that he'd told her he would see her soon? I hoped we wouldn't have to hang out with her. I hoped she wasn't going to be with us for dinner.

Faux Pa unlocked the car doors, and I got into the passenger seat. I watched him turn the key in the ignition and buckle his seat belt. For some reason Faux Pa always buckles his seat belt after he's started the car. "I'll try and take you here every couple of weeks until your mom gets back," he said.

"What will happen when Mom gets back?" I asked.

"It's impossible to say for sure," he said. "Right now

your grandmother can still have conversations with people, but a year is a long time for her." A year seemed like a long time for anyone. This time last year my life had been completely different.

Mom was losing her mother—Grandma was becoming less and less like the person she used to be. *Leigh who?* Grandma had said.

Mom still loved Grandma because she remembered what Grandma used to be like. The weird thing was that I had sort of lost my mother too. She was different than I'd thought she was, but I could remember her from before, too. I wondered if Faux Pa thought about that, and loved Mom because of all the good memories. I wondered what life would be like for all of us this time next year.

"Do you think you'll marry Jocelyn again?" I asked Faux Pa. I just blurted it out. The second the words were out of my mouth, I couldn't believe I'd said them.

"What?" Faux Pa asked. "What made you think of that?"

"I don't know," I said, even though I knew exactly what had made me think it. Lately, he smiled when he talked to Jocelyn on the phone, and she'd come to lunch that day. Maybe she was the reason he was willing to spend money at a restaurant. It was possible he was falling back in love with her. I had a horrible fear that Faux Pa would divorce Mom and remarry Jocelyn. I wondered what that would make Jocelyn to me? My step-stepmother? "I guess it would just make sense," I told him. "Jessa and Justin are your real kids, after all."

"You're my real kid, too," he said.

"Not biologically," I reminded him. "I don't even call you Dad."

"It doesn't matter what you call me," he said. "I'm

your father, and to answer your question—no, absolutely not. I'm not going to marry Jocelyn again. We didn't work together—at least not as a married couple."

"Are you going to divorce Mom, too?" I asked. After all, they hadn't worked together as a married couple, at least not since Mom was arrested.

"I don't know," Faux Pa said. "I love her, but I'm angry with her. I don't know what's going to happen."

"I hate not knowing what's going to happen," I said.

"I know this is hard for you," Faux Pa said. "You've been such a trooper."

"I don't feel like a trooper," I said.

"You've been great," Faux Pa said. He stopped at a red light and turned to me. "I'm really lucky you're my daughter."

"I'm really lucky you're my faux pa," I said.

Behind us someone was honking. The light had turned green. Faux Pa turned back to face the road. "We'll make it to West Virginia in the next few weeks," he told me. "It's a long drive, so we'll have to plan a weekend around it. I'll look into hotel prices. In the meantime, tomorrow we can do anything you want. Justin has an evening game, but the day is yours. We can go to a movie—even a chick flick—though I'd prefer to go to a matinee to save some money."

"Justin would hate to see a chick flick," I said.

"If that's what you want to do, Justin will deal with it," Faux Pa said. "And so will Jessa—she doesn't strike me as the kind of girl who would ordinarily see that kind of movie. But who knows? She did go shopping with you a couple weeks ago."

Right then I knew what I wanted to do, but even

though Faux Pa said we could do whatever I wanted, I wasn't sure he would let me.

"There is something," I said.

"Name it, and we'll do it," he said.

"You're not going to like it," I said.

"Try me," Faux Pa said.

"I want to go to the mall," I told him.

"Oh, honey, I'm sorry. I know you loved shopping with your mother, but we can't spend like that right now. We really have to watch our money."

"Ally Jaron's going to be there," I said. "I don't want to shop. I just want to talk to her."

We pulled up in front of Jocelyn's house. Faux Pa turned off the engine, but he didn't move to get out of thc car. "I understand why you want to speak to her," he said. It was funny because I didn't really understand it myself. The last time I'd talked to her, she'd rushed me off the phone. But Annie and I had made up, so maybe Ally and I would too. I just had this feeling that I'd been handed that flyer for a reason. It was the kind of thing Ally's guru would say. Maybe I was meant to get it, and meant to go back to the mall to see her.

"Why don't you sleep on it?" Faux Pa suggested. "If you still want to go in the morning, then I'll take you. Is that fair?"

"Yeah," I said. "Thanks."

"Okay," he said. He pressed the horn a couple times, quickly. A few seconds later the front door opened, and Jessa and Justin came out to the car.

chapter twenty-seven

When I was about seven years old, Mom brought me to a *Lovelock Falls* event in Manhattan. It was at Chelsea Piers, a huge complex by the Hudson River. There's a ballroom next to a pier, and there were hundreds—maybe thousands—of people packed in, waiting to meet the cast of *Lovelock Falls*. Mom and I were holding hands, weaving our way through the crowd. I was holding a bottle of water, and I guess I wasn't gripping it tightly enough because it slipped out of my hand. I let go of Mom and bent down to get it. It was just a second. Someone stepped in front of me, and when I stood up to look for Mom, she was gone.

I screamed for her, but there were so many people, and she didn't hear me. No one seemed to notice me, even though I was crying. I was shorter than everyone else, and I was lost in the crowd. I went around and around, looking for anything that was a sign of

Mom—her purple sweater dress, her brown leather purse, her hair, her arm. Nothing was familiar. I got to the front of the room. Ally was in a booth, signing autographs. I squeezed my way past the people waiting for her. "Carly!" she said. "What happened?"

"I lost my mom," I sobbed.

Ally asked someone for a microphone. "Can I please have everyone's attention? I have an announcement to make." She waited for the crowd to quiet down before she continued. It was amazing how everyone just stopped to listen to her. "Leigh Wheeler, please report to Ally Jaron. I have your daughter."

Right before us the crowd seemed to part, and then there was Mom, rushing toward us. She swept me up in her arms, and I wept into her shoulder. "It's okay," she said. "I'm right here."

That was what I was thinking about when Faux Pa pulled up in front of Neiman Marcus to drop Jessa and me off. He and Justin were going to park the car and meet us later, in the food court across the mall. I opened the car door and stepped outside. The air was cool. My heart was pumping really fast. Jessa and I walked up the steps toward the store. Through the windows I could see a crowd of people. I started to think that the whole thing was a really bad idea.

"Are you okay?" Jessa asked.

I nodded. I had to remind myself how to put one foot in front of the other, to walk forward. Jessa pulled open the door, and we walked inside, into the shoe department. It's on the first floor near the cosmetics.

"Whoa," Jessa said. "It's like a madhouse in here. I can't believe how many people showed up just to meet some actress from a soap opera."

Right then a girl came running past us and threw her arms around a woman—maybe her mother—who was waiting for her next to the Manolo Blahnik shoes. "Oh my God, I met her! I actually met her! She was so nice. She talked to me just like I was her friend. I really wanted to invite her to come to lunch with us!" The girl was waving Ally's head shot in the air like a pom-pom, and I recognized the picture. Mom had helped Ally pick out clothing for the photo shoot.

Jessa leaned toward me. "I don't understand people who are so obsessed with celebrities like that." She paused for a second. "Obviously, I don't mean you—I know that's not why you wanted to come here."

"It's okay," I said.

"Where is she, anyway?"

I stood on my tiptoes, but it was hard to see anything through the crowd. "Probably somewhere over there near the perfume section."

"Are you ready?" Jessa asked, and I nodded.

We made our way through the crowd, bumping into people as we went. I spotted Ally behind a makeup counter. She extended her arm to hand something to a girl in front of her, and I saw she was wearing an orange blouse with ruffled sleeves. "Jessa, look, there she is," I said.

A woman tugged on my arm. "Excuse me, missy, there's a line," she said.

"It's okay," Jessa said. "We're just here to say hello."

Someone with a name tag that read DEIDRE walked by us. The woman flagged her down. "They're trying to cut the line," she said, nodding toward Jessa and me.

Back in lower school kids used to tell on each other like that in the cafeteria. It was funny to hear a grown woman say it about Jessa and me. I wanted Ally to see me right then. I imagined her calling out my name, the way she had at the Chelsea Piers event. Then the tattling woman would know I was important; I wasn't just another fan. But then again it was possible that Ally wouldn't want to see me this time at all.

"Girls," the woman with the DEIDRE name tag said, "we're aiming for organized chaos here, so we really need you to get on line. If you want an autographed picture, give me your name and I'll write it on a sticky note so you can hand it up to Ms. Jaron."

"Elisabeth," the tattletale said quickly, I guess to make sure we didn't butt in and get our sticky notes first. "With an *s*—E-L-I-S-A-B-E-T-H."

"And that's why we have the stickies," Deidre said, "to make sure Ms. Jaron spells your name correctly when she autographs the photo." She turned to Jessa and me. "What about you, girls?"

"I don't need a picture," I said. I had plenty of them. At least I used to. They were boxed up in our house somewhere. "I know her."

"Everyone here thinks they know her," Deirdre said. Her voice was nice but firm. "You still have to wait on line."

Elisabeth-with-an-s looked back at us smugly. Jessa and I walked to the back of the line. All around us people were talking about Ally. You could feel how excited and nervous they were. The girl in front of us was saying how she wanted to be Violet van Ryan when she grew up. It was a really stupid thing to say—after all, Violet van Ryan isn't even a real person, and her made-up life is pretty crazy, between her near-death experiences, all of her divorces, and her evil twin sister. But there was a part of me that understood what the girl meant, because no matter what happened to Violet, she still seemed fabulous. She just smiled, and everyone loved her. I wished I could be like that. Even Annie wasn't like that, not completely. She was still popular at school, but she had lost something. People weren't as afraid of her anymore.

The line was taking a really long time, and I was worried we'd gotten there too late, that Ally would leave before it was our turn. Maybe I wasn't meant to see Ally after all. Or maybe her guru was wrong, and things didn't happen for a reason—they just happened.

And then, suddenly, we were almost at the front. The scent of perfume was heavy in the air. It was flowery, but not really in a pleasant way. It smelled like I was being suffocated by flowers. There were only three people ahead of us. I could hear Ally's voice, and my heart was pounding harder and harder. I wondered if Jessa could hear it. Ally was saying good-bye to the girls in front of us, but they clearly didn't want to leave her. "It was great to meet you," Ally said. "Hope to see you again someday."

Jessa pushed me forward. "It's your turn," she said.

I looked up at Ally, and she looked up at me. Our eyes met, but I felt frozen. I was scared she would tell me to go away.

"Carly," she said.

"Hi, Ally," I said. She looked beautiful, the way she always did. I wondered who had picked out her outfit for the day. I swallowed so I wouldn't start to cry.

"What a surprise," Ally said.

"I was here a couple weeks ago and I saw the flyer," I told her.

Ally held her hand out toward Jessa. "You must be a friend of Carly's," she said. "I'm Ally Jaron."

"I'm Jessa," Jessa said. "I'm Carly's stepsister."

"Oh, I've heard about you," Ally said. "Leigh told me she had stepchildren." It was strange to hear Ally say Mom's name. Somehow I just hadn't expected it. "It's really nice to meet you."

"It's nice to meet you, too," Jessa said.

"I've been thinking about you, Carly," Ally said.

"Really?" I asked. She nodded. "I've been thinking about you, too," I said. "How are you? How are the girls?"

"We're all good. The girls are growing up so fast I can hardly believe it. Madison cut her hair off, so it's just above her shoulders. I didn't want her to do it, but it looks so cute. And Nicole is getting into ice skating now. She has her first exhibition coming up, so she's really excited about it."

"I wish I could see them," I said.

"I know you do," Ally said. Right then I wished so hard that it could all go back to the way it used to be—when she used to like my mother, and she would invite me over when I asked about the girls. We were quiet for a moment, and it felt like something was caught between us. "Listen, do you girls want to test out the perfume or get an autographed picture?" Ally asked. "That's really what I'm here for today."

I shook my head. "No, thanks," I said.

"I'm sorry, Carly," Ally said. "I didn't expect to see you here."

"Are you mad at me for coming?" I asked.

"Of course I'm not mad," Ally said. "I was never mad at you, and I'm sorry I rushed you off the phone that day. It's just . . . sometimes things happen, and you can't be friends. I know it's not fair. It's just the way it is. I'll always care about you. Things are just different now."

I thought about how delicate friendships can be, like being popular. It can all disappear, even when you haven't done anything wrong. Maybe Mom deserved to lose Ally, but I didn't. And yet I knew Ally wasn't trying to be mean to me. "I hate my mom for what she did," I said. "She ruined everything."

"Oh, Carly," Ally said.

"It's okay," I said, even though it wasn't. "I guess I just came here to say good-bye. We never got to say good-bye."

Ally stood up and came around the counter. She enveloped me in a hug. It was probably the last time I'd see her, and I knew I would always remember it. I smelled perfume on her that was sweet and light, and I realized she wasn't even wearing the perfume she was trying to sell. "Good-bye, honey," she said.

"Good-bye," I said.

Ally shook Jessa's hand again, which made me jealous. For some reason, I wanted to be the person that Ally touched last. But I knew it would be weird for me to go up to her again. Jessa and I started to walk away. "I've been waiting to meet you my whole life," I heard someone behind me say.

"Wait, Carly," Ally called. "Come back here a second."

I turned around. The girl who had been in line behind us looked annoyed that Ally was paying attention to me instead of her. She was probably jealous that Ally knew my name. If only she knew why.

I walked up to the counter. Ally reached for my hand. "Do you know what my guru says the secret to happiness is?" she asked.

I shook my head. "No," I said. "What?"

"Forgiveness," she said. "When you talk to your mom, tell her I said that."

"I will," I said. Ally squeezed my hand and let it go. Then I led Jessa out of Neiman Marcus and through the mall to the food court.

chapter twenty-eight

We went to visit Mom the next weekend. Faux Pa picked me up from school on Friday, our overnight bags already in the backseat, and we drove to West Virginia.

He had made reservations for us to stay at a motel about a half hour away from Camp Petunia. Finally, after nine hours in the car, we pulled into the parking lot of a Holiday Inn. Ordinarily, I would've been excited about spending a night in a motel—I love the mini soaps and bottles of shampoo they leave in the bathroom, and I love how someone comes in to make your bed every day. But it was different, knowing Mom was sleeping in a bunk bed a few miles away, in prison. There were two double beds in our room, and Faux Pa let me choose which one I wanted to sleep in. I picked the one by the window, and he got the one closer to the bathroom. He set the alarm on the nightstand between our beds. Visiting hours started at eight a.m., so we were going to wake up at seven, as if it were a school day and not a weekend.

In the morning the alarm went off, a soft steady buzz. At first it seemed like part of my dream. But then I heard Faux Pa say, "Sugar," and the sounds of the sheets crinkling as he sat up in the bed next to me. He reached to turn the alarm clock off. Suddenly, I remembered where I was, and I was wide awake.

Faux Pa went into the bathroom to shower and change. When he was done, I brought my stuff into the bathroom. I unwrapped the complimentary shower cap so I could shower without getting my hair wet.

"I'm going to see Mom today," I said out loud. The water was running, so Faux Pa couldn't hear me, otherwise I would've been embarrassed to be caught talking to myself. But I felt like I needed to say it out loud to believe it. It had been more than four weeks since I'd seen her. Four weeks and five days. That made it thirty-three days total. I wondered if I would ever stop counting how long it had been since Mom had been sent away. It seemed like the sort of thing I'd keep track of until the day she came home. She had missed a lot, in just over a month, and so much more would happen before her sentence was over. I didn't know what life would be like this time next year; I didn't even know where I'd be living or going to school. But I knew it was never going to go back to normal, to the way it used to be. It was like how things were still different between Annie and me, even though we'd made up, because we'd learned things about each other. I'd learned things about Mom, too.

Right then, I knew what Ally had meant when she'd said forgiveness was the secret to happiness.

When I came out of the bathroom, Faux Pa was putting his driver's license and some cash into a ziplock bag, like a sandwich bag. "Why are you doing that?" I asked.

"It's one of the prison rules," he explained. "You need to bring your things in a plastic bag so the prison officials can see through them and make sure you're not bringing in any contraband."

"Like something to pick the locks with?"

"Right, or a weapon of some sort," he said. I shuddered when he said that. I couldn't imagine Mom with a weapon. "Do you have a school ID?"

"Yeah," I said. "It's in my backpack. Why?"

"The rules on the prison website say everyone needs to bring an ID," Faux Pa said. "I'm sure kids are the exception, but bring it along just in case."

We left the motel a few minutes later and got back into the car. We drove along a winding road. There weren't too many houses in Fairlawn, West Virginia. I guess people didn't want to live too close to a prison. It felt like we were in the middle of nowhere. We made a turn past a sign that said FEDERAL PRISON CAMP, and pulled up to the front gate. Faux Pa rolled down his window and gave his name to the man in the booth. Then the gate lifted and we continued onto the prison grounds. There was a long, red brick building and then a couple of other, smaller buildings. We drove around the back of the big building to the visitors' parking lot. I saw a basketball court and a track. It could've been a school campus.

We got out of the car and walked across a wide lawn to the front entrance. There was a line forming out front—men, women, and children waiting to get into the prison. We didn't talk to each other, even though we all had this thing in common. I mean, I didn't know anyone else who had ever had to visit anyone in prison.

There was a whole process to getting into the prison. It was sort of like when you go to the airport, when they have to check to make sure you're really the person whose name is on the ticket. We waited on line. When it was our turn, Faux Pa showed the guard our IDs. The guard checked to make sure our names were on the list of people allowed to visit Mom. Afterward we got a list of the prison rules, like no gifts and no running. Then we had to sign a form acknowledging we'd read the rules. We had to put our jackets and the car keys in a locker. Finally, we were allowed back to the visitors' room.

It looked like a cafeteria. There were tables with benches. The prisoners were all dressed the same—blue uniforms and black boots. There were prison guards stationed around the room. It was strange, because Mom couldn't even be alone in a room with Faux Pa and me. There were so many people around us. I scanned the benches for Mom. It was hard to pick her out, since the prison uniform wasn't anything she would normally wear.

And then I saw her. She was standing by a bench on the left side of the room. I could tell she saw me at the same time that I saw her, because her face changed. It went from a kind of blank stare to a wide smile. I wanted to run to her, but I knew it was against the rules. I didn't want to be kicked out.

I walked as quickly as I could. Mom's eyes were shiny. I knew I was crying, because my cheeks were wet. She opened up her arms. The rules said we were allowed to hug her at the beginning and end of our visit, and I fell in to her. She held me tightly and rocked me. I hoped we weren't hugging for longer than we were allowed. When we let go, Faux Pa stepped forward and hugged her hello too. It was very quick. I wiped my face and tried to figure out what it meant—he hugged her, so that was good. But I knew he was still mad at her.

"Should we sit down?" Faux Pa asked.

"Yes, I think that's what we're supposed to do," Mom said. She held out her arm like she was welcoming us into her home. "So this is Camp Petunia. I hope you brought your gardening shears."

Mom was making jokes, and we sat down at the table. I sat down next to her, and Faux Pa was on the other side. The rules didn't say anything about not being able to sit next to Mom. I glanced over at the prison guard standing the closest to us. She was standing against the wall with her arms folded across her chest. She looked serious but not particularly angry.

"Oh, Carly, I found something out the other day, and I've been so excited to tell you. A new inmate was assigned to kitchen duty yesterday—she was convicted for tax evasion—and she has a daughter your age, so we have that in common. That's her over there."

I looked to where Mom was pointing. Across the room there was a woman with dark hair pulled back in a ponytail. Except for the prison uniform she looked like a completely ordinary woman.

"Her name is Fran," Mom continued. "You'll never guess what she told me yesterday."

"What?" I asked.

"I told her about your name, and how we sometimes try to figure out what Carly Simon meant when she said her dreams were clouds in her coffee. And Fran told me that she once read an article about it. Carly Simon herself explained that she was on an airplane drinking coffee, and she could see the clouds from outside the window reflected in her cup of coffee. Can you believe that? After all those theories we came up with, there were literal clouds in her coffee!"

I shook my head. "That's so simple," I said. "It almost doesn't make sense."

"I know," Mom said. She looked at me and shook her head, like she couldn't quite believe I was really there. "It's just so good to see you," she said. "To see both of you."

"It's good to see you, too," I told her.

"You look well," Faux Pa said.

Mom nodded. "I know I screwed up and I deserve this," she said. "But you don't—neither of you—and I'm really sorry."

"You're right about that, Leigh," Faux Pa said. He was still angry. I didn't feel that way anymore.

"Mom," I said, "there's something I have to tell you."

"What, honey?"

I took a deep breath. I was thinking about what Mrs. Sarsen had told Mom: *You're still my friend.* Mom was also still my mom. I loved her, and I forgave her.

"I forgive you," I said. I started to smile. As soon as I said the words, I knew I really meant them.

"Oh, honey," Mom said, her eyes shining, "you don't know how much that means to me."

I wanted to hug her, but of course I wasn't allowed

to until the end of the visit. I looked over at Faux Pa, and he smiled at me. Nothing that had happened had been erased. Maybe he would never forgive Mom. But still, Ally was right: There was this feeling of peace and happiness inside me. It felt so big and important, like it was filling up every space inside me, all the things I had been and was now, and all I would ever be.